A WANDER IN THE WOODS

2021

Delightful Tales

Edited By Byron Tobolik

First published in Great Britain in 2021 by:

 Young**Writers**®
— Est. 1991 —

Young Writers
Remus House
Coltsfoot Drive
Peterborough
PE2 9BF
Telephone: 01733 890066
Website: www.youngwriters.co.uk

Printed and bound in the UK by BookPrintingUK
Website: www.bookprintinguk.com
YB0473E

FOREWORD

Welcome, Reader!

Are you ready to take a Wander in the Woods? Then come right this way - your journey to amazing adventures awaits. It's very simple, all you have to do is turn the page and you'll be transported into a forest brimming with super stories.

Is it magic? Is it a trick? No! It's all down to the skill and imagination of primary school pupils from around the country. We gave them the task of writing a story and to do it in just 100 words! I think you'll agree they've achieved that brilliantly – this book is jam-packed with exciting and thrilling tales, and such variety too, from mystical portals to creepy monsters lurking in the dark!

These young authors have brought their ideas to life using only their words. This is the power of creativity and it gives us life too! Here at Young Writers we want to pass our love of the written word onto the next generation and what better way to do that than to celebrate their writing by publishing it in a book!

It sets their work free from homework books and notepads and puts it where it deserves to be – out in the world and preserved forever! Each awesome author in this book should be super proud of themselves, and now they've got proof of their ideas and their creativity in black and white, to look back on in years to come!

CONTENTS

Independent Entries

Safiya Parsons	70	Emily Silver (8)	113
Zain Ahmed (10)	71	Aryan Yadav (11)	114
Asha Webster (10)	72	Aarush Ram	115
Rebecca Morrison (8)	73	Ishba Huq	116
Kayla Culley	74	Sophia Simmons	117
Guillem Bonet (6)	75	Dua Umer (11)	118
Matilda Anthopoulos (8)	76	Chisomeje Emeka-Gwacham (8)	119
Kinza Naveed	77	Zainab Afsar (11)	120
Gabriel Spencer-Bird	78	Aima Saqib (10)	121
Khadija Adams (8)	79	Shofei Shanthakumar (8)	122
Umika Singh (8)	80	Liliana O'Mallo	123
Inaya Javed (10)	81	Jasmine Kaur Gill (11)	124
Kiya Bhatt (10)	82	Pooja Koripalli (7)	125
Emilia Pennie (10)	83	Saveen Wickramaratne (9)	126
Sulaimaan Mohammed (10)	84	Aditya Bassan (7)	127
Elysia Barno (10)	85	Suveethan Sureshkumar (9)	128
Chantelle Nakintu Mwanje	86	Eliza Aroush Ehjaz (9)	129
Sayali Joglekar (11)	87	Sophie Goodwin (11)	130
Keira Brown	88	Madison Bebb (11)	131
Ali Nagey (9)	89	Anya Joy (10)	132
Heritage Agbaje (9)	90	Rebecca Maling (10)	133
Manreet Kaur (10)	91	Subhan Khalid (9)	134
Sofia McMillan (8)	92	Sumera Arshad (11)	135
Dhieshaa Sureshkumar (8)	93	Georgia Duncan	136
Lillian May Pedley (12)	94	Emelia Hanson (10)	137
Tayyib Patel (9)	95	Lola-Mai Nicholls	138
Amelia Szaja (10)	96	Kashish Gupta (8)	139
Tenzin Phuntsok (11)	97	Keya Joshi	140
Anabia Javed (8)	98	Gabriela Nakova (7)	141
Scarlett Dowkes (9)	99	Poppy Smith	142
Jasmine Davies (10)	100	Willow Silver (8)	143
Diya Jain (10)	101	Florence Coen (10)	144
Namyaa Singhal (10)	102	Kyra Dixon (8)	145
Anaiah Da Cunha (10)	103	Shazim Aamir (7)	146
Jonathan Miller (8)	104	Claudia Castley (8)	147
Nicole Abitimo Oloya (8)	105	Javeria Khan (10)	148
Likya Meis Bultan (8)	106	Merryn Walker (9)	149
Chinmayi Reghunath	107	Rebecca Ajibade (8)	150
Sophie Bellwood (9)	108	Sasi Vadan Vemu (7)	151
Mariam Imran	109	Zara Imran (9)	152
Luis Gjoka (10)	110	Megan Ward (10)	153
James Morrissey (10)	111	Shiloh Elisabeth Vijayendran	154
Trisha Varkey (9)	112	Mia Martin (9)	155

Keya Bhundia (9)	156	Oliver Barford (11)	199
Michael Barua	157	Eshaal Mudassar	200
Brooklyn Smith	158	Harriet Jeffery (8)	201
Pin-Chieh Chou (9)	159	Ethan Alphonse	202
Xander Withcrow	160	Sebastian Nodsle (8)	203
Keira Garrs (10)	161	Gurnaman Singh	204
Zainab Akter	162	Lucy Rowe (11)	205
Eleni Symeonidou (11)	163	Elektra Thomas (10)	206
Adyan Shahzad	164	Enzo Wilson	207
Nehan Illagolla (7)	165	Alfie Warriner	208
Eva Bray (8)	166	Alexia Nyathi (7)	209
Areeba Waqas (9)	167	James Ireland	210
Millie Miller	168		
Walter D'Olier (7)	169		
Sophie Salmon	170		
Cressida Bird (9)	171		
Thanya Uruthrasingam (10)	172		
Lily Shufflebottom	173		
Mhairi MacDonald (9)	174		
Peter Daley (11)	175		
Sahasra Veerammagari (10)	176		
Alice Peng (7)	177		
Luke Tang	178		
Isabelle Usher (10)	179		
Liam Kew	180		
Aretha Tsanga (10)	181		
Azlan Khalid Noor (9)	182		
Amara Mankodi (9)	183		
Rosie Elliott	184		
Edmund Mwanje (10)	185		
Tony White (9)	186		
Lilly Copley (9)	187		
Charlie Turner	188		
Ella-Dhiya Chauhan	189		
Maryam K (10)	190		
Sura Lilly (11)	191		
Vinudi Gigurawa Gamage (7)	192		
Shereen George	193		
Aaron Willis (10)	194		
Sammy Norman (11)	195		
Renah Tamara	196		
Jack Jakaj (9)	197		
Betty Brocklesby Sum (10)	198		

THE
STORIES

Goblin Adventure

The fire was crackling; it was time for an enchanting story. It was getting dark. In the distance, I saw a huge, never-ending tree. Did anyone know what was at the top? Apparently, not me. I looked around. I could see fairy goblins, a dwarf, bizarre creatures. I took a moment, rubbed my eyes, whispering, "Am I dreaming?"

"No," the goblin muttered.

"Arghh! Did you just talk?"

"Yes," replied the goblin.

"I have to get out of here."

"First, you must help us find the dwarf's underpants, Fairy Twinkle's precious dust and Goblin's spaceship!"

"Haha," I chuckled. "Wait, you're serious?"

Amelia Butt (9)

The Vanishing

"But... Mum, I don't want to!" His eyes sparkled with sadness.

"Noah, please go to the woods with your dad to hunt for food."

He hated going into the woods at dusk.

"Son, you stay on the lookout."

Noah sighed, "Yes, Dad!" He trudged around, bored. Sadness consumed him.

Bang!

"What was that?"

Noah struggled to speak, he noticed his dad had vanished. "I need to find Dad," he panicked. He traced their footprints home.

"Mum, where's Dad?"

Noah's mum replied, "Dad? He died years ago!"

Confusion swamped Noah. "You must have imagined him?"

Or did he?

Rebecca Iona (9)

The Boy In The Woods

Jake was still running aimlessly through the forest looking for food in the dark. Jake was the lively, energetic offspring of a poverty-stricken couple. Jake might've looked like the happiest child but deep down inside, he was devastated watching his parents struggle. Attempting to help, he decided to look for food however it was hopeless. Then something mysterious and miraculous happened. A cute bunny hopped forward and shockingly disappeared. Jake inquisitively chased after the bonny and was immediately transported to an amazing, magical land. Mesmerised by the glorious sight, he invited his parents, and their long-suffering was finally over.

Darren John (10)

The Notorious Noise...

I heard a noise behind me. From the trunk of a tree, an oak tree. *How bizarre*, I thought. There was never anything of that sort in Beechview Woods, not ever. There it was again, that thing squawking.

"Is that a bird?" I queried. This time, aloud. My pale, confused, terrified face looked around. Nothing. Nothing in sight. Where was the animal-sounding thing? *Squawk!*

"Where is that horrid-sounding thingamajig?" The animal squawked and squawked, even more, every single minute. Suddenly, something flew into sight. It landed on my extended arm.

"Well, hello, little thing! Come with me, uhh, Stella."

Ibteda Mahmud (10)

Instinct

"Are you sure, Laurelle? Aunty says that the forest is off-limits." Wisdom was trailing behind, her nose in a book.

"Yes, I jolly well am sure!" Laurelle was skipping ahead.

"What if there is no flower?"

"I am pretty sure there is!" Laurelle was pointing at a golden flower that was covered in ivy. A wolf howled. An invisible clock began to tick.

"Asmundr really did curse this forest and he really did want to destroy Euclides."

"We shouldn't be here, Laurelle, please."

"If we could take it-" *Crack!* An ear-splitting scream. Then silence.

Pippa Barlow (10)

The Ghost And Siblings

Once upon a time, there were two siblings called Raneeda and Shoz. They were very kind. Nervously, they went to the forest by themselves. Suddenly, the siblings felt something and then they got scared; it felt like someone or something was following them! Shaking, Raneeda said, "Hello, is anybody there?"

Suddenly, a ghost appeared. They both yelled but didn't move. As fast as a cheetah, the ghost said, "I want to be your friend."

They both stopped yelling and said, "Are you a deadly ghost?"

The ghost said, "No."

Then Shoz said, "Want to be our friend?"

"Yes!"

Adeena Siar (8)

Greedy Goldilocks

Once, a sweet girl walked through woodland as the wind blew softly through her fair hair. Suddenly, she saw a cottage decorated with tempting sweets. She knocked on the door twice. No reply. On the third knock, she entered...

Inside, she gasped at shimmering, sugary delights and scrumptious cakes. She grabbed handfuls. As she took a bite, a huge howl vibrated through the cottage...

"Who's been gobbling up my cakes?" growled a bear, confronting the terrified Goldilocks. It hurtled towards her. The creature clawed at her. She screamed. It bit. She metamorphosed.

Now, two grizzled beasts protect the candy-witch's cottage.

William Layton

Gruesome Ghosts

The weird, white, floating figures were still after us. "Elizabeth!" I yelled, "They're catching up with us!" We ran until we could run no more and found ourselves outside my home. "We'll be safe here." I could never have been more wrong because the gruesome ghosts poured in through the doors like milk out of a jug. They waved their swords around everywhere feeling for us. Suddenly, I heard a shrieking voice. "Isabelle!" screamed Elizabeth, "Save meee!" And that was the last I ever saw of my best friend. She would spend the rest of her life as a ghost.

Nusaybah Bint-Khalid (10)

A Mysterious Encounter

One tempestuous, turbulent morning, Tom was walking by the dark, dim woods until he came to an abrupt halt. In front of him, there was a gargantuan, hungry dragon with sharp, shimmering teeth. Tom's jaw dropped and sweat came running down his face at a blistering pace. The dragon opened its bloodshot, bulging, ravenous eyes with rancid breath and diabolical grin, craving to gorge on Tom. Tom coughed loudly. The trees rumbled. The dragon leapt hungrily, but Tom dashed out like a bullet. Petrified Tom and the dejected, famished dragon thought to themselves, *this is the worst encounter of my life!*

Vihaan Arora (8)

A Place Of Fear!

It was getting dark when Raphael strolled through the woods. The trees started to look like skeletons' hands reaching towards him, grabbing whatever was lurking below them. It looked like a leafy graveyard falling to the depths of the earth, silently waiting, sitting patiently for trespassers to come by and pounce when they were near. Blossom on the trees had dispersed and they were chained with iron bars, covered in moss underneath a shade of pitch-black darkness. The woods were horrifying and murky. The trees were the leaves' haunted friends and the grass was disappearing like a popped balloon...

Jamie Tyrrell (8)

Hermopolis

It was getting dark. We had to get out of there. "Here, let's swap Hermopolis," Cairo muttered, twisting off the ring in his hand and handing it to me. I took off my earrings and did the same.

"Drix wings on," I breathed.

"Griff, let's fly," Cairo whispered.

The barbarians barely noticed anything. Wow, now that I look back, the fools! We quickly untied ourselves, but one of them noticed and I guess it was one of the smartest, Mira, now that I know their names. She pointed at us.

"Urgh, urgh, urghhh! Escaped, we've escaped 'em!" We were caught...

Megan Joshi (9)

The Mist Of The Night

"This is the forest, right?" exclaimed Trixy. Her voice echoed through the woods. As all of the three children walked one by one the breeze from the wind gave them the chills. Leaves rustled, trees swayed. The forest was silent. They were all worried especially the youngest, Winita. They knew that this was a horrible idea once they had entered the forest.

Suddenly a dark woman's figure walked up and spoke, "You must leave this forest - now."

They all ran not knowing where they were heading until they stumbled across an old, rusty, haunted house. They were completely lost.

Holly Bolaji (10)

The Mysterious Jungle

The trees were creaking eerily. The wind was screaming through their branches when a human-like creature with the head of an ox ran like a cheetah towards me, but I somehow managed to dodge it. While swerving through trees, I came across the kingdom of such harmless organisms who mesmerised me with their altruism. To my despair, they narrated that a behemoth with wings like an enormous eagle devoured them every day. After continuous motivation and encouragement, meticulous planning helped us defeat the giant and brought his brutality to an end. Overwhelmed, I was crowned their king. Then I woke up.

Parth Aggarwal (10)

The Creature Behind The Tree

Kelly said goodbye to her auntie. She noticed a path that led through the dense trees. Slowly, she began stepping into a clearing. She found the remains of a fire. Kelly knew that something had been there. She began to run. Then she heard a snap. *Roar!* Kelly knew it was too late, she was going to be eaten. She had to run faster. Arms grabbed her waist. Kelly looked behind her and saw her auntie. Kelly exclaimed, "It's you!" Auntie replied, "I'm going to eat you!" Kelly screamed. "Not really!"

They all lived happily (until it happened again!).

Lola Tash (9)

An Eerie Camping Trip

In a dense forest, a group of friends were camping together. Little did they know, something was stalking them... The group were getting into their pyjamas when Harry saw something quite strange. He went to investigate, torch in hand and bravery rushing through him.

An hour had passed and he wasn't back. Everyone was scared. Nobody knew what to do. Eventually, they went to look for him, sticking together like glue. They wandered around the forest before finally finding their friend nestled in a tree, sleeping soundly.

In the end, they cut their trip short and never went camping again!

Isla Williams (10)

The Mysterious Monster

Between the village and the sea, lay a gigantic, gloomy grove. The villagers who travelled there never returned.

Early one morning, a village boy called Adak wandered into the grove where he discovered a sphinx! The sphinx smiled menacingly and said, "Answer this riddle to survive. It runs over the woods all day, under the bed at night, sits not alone. With a long tongue hanging out, what am I?"

Adak pondered the riddle. About to give up he looked down in despair, then he realised, "The answer's a shoe!" he exclaimed. Furious, the sphinx threw himself into the sea.

Luke Denford

An Obscure Rendezvous

Impenetrable clouds blocked out the starry heavens. Below, the valley was plunged into blackness; sinister silence settled in. I crashed through thickets of gnarled undergrowth. In the impenetrable gloom, my eyes strained for the carved symbols of the trees and I had to feel my way to our meeting place. Suddenly, I emerged into a clearing. Eerie silhouettes crept all about and cold mist swirled in around my ankles. Harrowing cries echoed loudly off the withered trees and the distorted outlines of stalking creatures danced past. Was this the rendezvous point? It was difficult to be sure in the dark.

Yuna Vavrovsky (11)

An Orphan's Dream

As helpless as a shipwrecked sailor, Elfin the orphan wandered through the woods. Feeling lost and forlorn, he could hear the faint, distinctive voices of his parents. In desperation, he darted his head around, but only birds caught his eye. Descending from the mist, Elfin saw his parents smiling at him from the far end. Elated that he'd found his parents, Elfin rushed towards them, eyes swimming in tears. Abruptly, they disappeared into the mist again. He shouted for them, which woke him up from his slumber.
"Mum, Dad, where are you? Elfin needs you..."
Sadness washed over him.

Lewis Le (10)

A Wander In The Woods

Sofia rushed through the streets, her energy ebbing from her heavy lungs. She checked her pale, silver-white watch racing in the crowded road. It was 9:07am! She gasped. She would be late for school! Chewing her tongue, she stopped to think. *There's the way through the woods or past Mr Mohammed's house which would be 30 minutes*, she pondered.

Finally, she took a deep breath, inhaling the babble of familiar and friendly smells and walked into the forest. Sofia stared at the mossy vines, muddy bank and tall, towering trees. She casually trotted in the drape of weak sunlight...

Muniba Yusuf (9)

The Enchanted Kirkwood Wonders

As they began approaching the mysterious woods, an invisible force pulled them deeper into the depths of dense and heavy woodland that lay ahead. Kirkwood, which was home to many monsters, spiders and other hideous beasts, was vibrant and colourful with paths full of glistening green grass. Its prominent features were the crimson sea of leaves and the gushing of the crystal clear waterfall mixed with the tweeting of birds. The deeper they entered the woods, their surroundings began to change. An eerie atmosphere flowed through the woods as if they were being hunted and summoned by a dark force...

Tasmiyah Maryam (11)

The 'Treesy' Secrets

The sun was setting. Darkness flooded around Janet and Isobel. They were horrified; how could their mother get lost? They were standing in the middle of a dingy wood, afraid to even breathe! They feared a ghost would shout, "Gotcha!" Then creep up behind them and grab them with its silver hands.

Suddenly, Janet curiously tiptoed towards a tree. A normal, mossy tree. No! A whispering tree! Quickly running towards Isobel, Janet pinched their arms very hard. "Ouch!" In the blink of an eye, a glistening light shone through the trees and the girls were back in their maths class.

Ronika Ghanaati (9)

The Stag In The Night

Living in the woods was extremely boring; every morning, birds sang their heartwarming melodies, trees rustled in the fresh breeze. Occasionally, I would see a little deer prancing along merrily. After an exhausting mooch, I ran upstairs and slumped down on my bed, immediately falling asleep. Eventually, I woke up to a glistening light in my window. I hastily jerked up and saw it... a navy blue stag standing proudly at the top of the hill. White stars painted here and there covered its body. From its antlers, were lanterns filled with the enchanting glow of every colour. It disappeared...

Sofia Rabbi (10)

Shadows In The Darkness

Crack! Something was behind me. Cautiously, I turned around, wondering what it was. "Who's there?" I murmured nervously. The eerie forest was becoming more mysterious by the second. A murder of crows squawked overhead and put my nerves on edge. Suddenly, I found myself in a deserted clearing and my body trembled. A shadow moved in the trees like a restless ghost. Cold sweat trickled down my forehead but I refused to give in to my fears. Rustling leaves caught my attention; it was coming closer! Leaping from the bushes, a golden dog came to the rescue. I'd been saved!

Georgia Begbey (10)

The Journey Through The Black Gates

Calmly, I walked through the black gates that led from an unknown forest into a completely new world... Confidence mounting, I walked through the gates. I felt a weird sensation flowing through my body. My throat tightened, my limbs loosened, my jaw gaped open. *Will it get any worse?* I asked myself. Gloom sank into me; I could not give up. I walked for hours until I met a carnivorous, nimble, panged, merciless creature. Horror choked me. I screamed, "Arghh!" What would I do? Before I could make my escape, the merciless monster grabbed my hand. What would happen next?

Aarya Patel (9)

Wander In The Woods

The cool breeze blew calmly through the flora as the leaves pirouetted down from the hickory trees which reached pridefully to the heavens. Filling the intoxicating air, fresh scents of flowers wafted up to my nose as I ventured deeper into the mystical forest. Flying wonders soared gracefully over my head, chirping in delight. A drop of glimmering dijon dew glissaded down my forehead before joining the squelching leaves below me. Emerging from a midday slumber, raccoons and rabbits skittered to an unknown destination, finding refuge in a tree log. My jaw dropped at God's creations.

Chayil John (10)

A Faint Shadow

Walking home alone in the ancient witches' wood, the sun started to set. I thought that I would take a different path back. All of a sudden, I stumbled across an old, creepy looking caravan. I was frightened, confused but also strangely curious. Without warning, the grubby curtains twitched... I quietly tiptoed closer and saw the door was open. Cautiously, I stepped inside... In one corner, a candle flickered. A faint shadow appeared. "Millie, is that you?" the whispering voice asked. The door shut. The candle blew out. Petrified, I was left in the pitch-blackness...

Millie Graves (12)

Through The Woods

Ahead of me, the forest was dark and silent. I'd no choice but to enter. It was a tangled maze with a never-ending journey. The damp smell of decaying, rotting leaves filled my senses. The branches swayed to the rhythm of the wind and their leaves fluttered like graceful butterflies. A spidery tangle of trees, bushes and gnarled limbs were cloaked in mist like ghostly, stooped figures.

Dead branches grasped my ankles and trapped them in a tight, thorny grasp. The sound of crying wolves, hooting owls and barking dogs created a sinister cacophony. When would this nightmare end?

Ishika Sharma (10)

A Journey To Home

She was running in the exotic woodland. She didn't have a torch. She tripped over a heavy stone and came through the metal tunnel. Rolling, rolling, tumbling and bumping into me. She screamed and cried, "I want to go home!"
"Don't worry, I will take you home," I said.
We climbed and climbed, finally coming to the entrance. A horrific, dreadful tree villain was there and started to chase us. We went over the river and ran onto the stones. He was close. We jumped over a gigantic tree. Suddenly, I fell off my bed. Where's Little Red Riding Hood?

Shiyam Thulasiraj (7)

A Twisted Hansel And Gretel Mini Saga

Once upon a time, Hansel and Gretel wandered into the enchanted woods. Hearing leaves crunch, they turned to see an evil-looking witch holding a bottle of glittering liquid. Quickly, the witch threw the liquid at the children. Suddenly, the wind swirled around them. The children were no longer good because the witch had turned them evil. Unexpectedly, the children grabbed the witch and took her to a cabin where they almost threw her into the oven! A magical phoenix came to the rescue. Seeing the children were not themselves, he gave them a cure. The children escaped on the phoenix.

Khadeja Shadoobuccus (8)

'Confessions' Of Red Riding Hood

I'm not like others. I can become anything. An enjoyable power.

One day, I see a wolf. A normal wolf padding through woodland. How boring! I'll make it a real wolf...

I wander through the deathly woods, arriving at the solitary shack where it sleeps. Shape-shifting from girl to wolf, I become the predator. Villagers hear my howls. The power creature cowers away from me. He knows who and what I really am...

I snarl. Growl. Howl. The real wolf whimpers. Villagers arrive with spears. I shift back. A poor, helpless girl! You hear the screams and howls for miles.

Hanna Zhang (9)

Soul Of Two

On the foggy horizon, I spotted a creepy figure dashing through the green forest. As any normal person would do, I just ignored it. I lived to regret that...

Weeks later, the eerie figure wasn't there in my vision. But suddenly, I heard a monstrous shriek behind my back. My heart had stopped and my body was petrified like a freeze-frame. I turned around and the aura of the mysterious creature was there haunting me. My soul was infinitely bound to it and my life had been changed.

This sinister monster has given me uncountable nightmares since that horrific day.

Andres Maduro (11)

Golden Cage

Blissful! The warm breeze stroked my cheeks gently, dappled sunbeams illuminated the path forward. The rippling brook flowed past; the chirps of soaring birds devoured the woods with melody. Squirrels scrambled nimbly, tree to tree, and fragrance from bloomed flowers consumed the atmosphere. Through the small gaps in the canopy above, a crystal blue sky seized my attention, making the canvas vibrant. If only this cage could be shattered to pieces and I could fly away. If only I could feel the wind beneath my wings. If only I could join in the melody of the chirping birds. If only!

Adrita Ghosh (11)

The Night I Met A Vampire

It was getting dark. I no longer felt alone in the woods. Something or someone was behind me. The warm night air turned ice-cold, the hairs on my arms stood up and the unsettling noises of tree branches snapping around me, made me nervous. *Poof!* Bulging, bloodshot eyes stared at me. It had bloodstained lips, razor-sharp fangs and was as pale as a ghost... a vampire. "I want to suck your blood!" he shrieked. He ran towards me, my heart pounding. Suddenly, he stopped and disappeared into the night. He must have smelt my garlicky breath! I am safe, for now.

Albie Dalley (8)

A Pathway To Something?

As I strolled through the enchanted woodland, the delicate pathway I was walking on had so many wonderful leaves that came flowing down, landing on me like feathers. Something nearly as bright as the sun caught my eye. This creature had huge, sage green wings that matched her Tinker Bell-like dress. Her lengthy, silky hair framed her small, pale face. Her tiny body was standing next to what looked like a minuscule rose-pink door that led into her treehouse. She was a fairy! Her gleam, shimmer and bewitching essence shone like the sun amongst the beautiful trees surrounding us.

Elise McFarlane (11)

A Girl Who Escaped The Forest

A girl called Lucy had a brother called Lewis. It was his bedtime but Lucy didn't have a story, so she went on an adventure. Suddenly, there was a portal. Lucy got sucked up... It was a haunted forest. Then a witch called Wendy came.

"Please let me go!" Lucy cried.

"You have to guess my favourite film," Wendy said.

"Umm, maybe the Joker?"

"No," said the witch.

"Revenge Tastes Sweet?"

She melted. Lucy was excited. She had defeated the witch. She was free and she had a story to tell her brother.

Titilolaoluwa Lawson (10)

A Woodland Wander

At the edge of town, there is a little plot of farmland where the sweetest of scents from the fresh crops lingers and the sky is always that lovely cornflower blue. If you cross it, you'll find woods. Follow the pathway lined with vibrant buds, berries and blooms and distinctive white roses that beckon you through the woods. Here, the rambling brambles seem to silently, over time, sneak everywhere. At the end of the pathway, you'll find an old, abandoned cabin with a cottage beside it with strange red roses spookily growing upwards. It is here that my story begins...

Alice Fowler (8)

The Forest Of Enchanted Wonders

A few streets from my ordinary home, there was a forest filled with only trees, tree stumps and leaves. "Go and take Mr Woofers to the forest, Emily," my mum said.

As I entered the forest, I saw a golden, luminous glow appearing from below a tree stump. Being a curious child, I touched it softly and blacked out. When I regained consciousness, I saw wonders. Trees made of gold, growing every jewel imaginable. Pansies of silver spreading around like a disease and bronze birds tweeting the sweetest, mesmerising music.

It was amazing there, but how would I get out...?

Tarnriya Johnson (11)

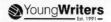
Olivia's Ruby Magic

A girl named Olivia was walking in the woods. She found a ruby on the ground and decided to bring it home. When she got home, "Olivia, what are you holding?"
Olivia stopped and said, "Nothing, I'm just angry about school."
Olivia's mum let her go up to her room. Olivia kept staring at the ruby. "I wonder if this ruby can do magic." The ruby started glowing. Olivia started flying and purple foam went around her. It all stopped and Olivia felt weird and started flying again, she also got laser eyes. She had superpowers for good.

Chloé Servan-Smalley

The Adventure Of Confused Ryan And Giant Gabby

It was getting dark in the spooky woods. Ryan and Gabby were camping. They were all alone. Soon, they fell asleep. All of a sudden, at 12am, guess what happened? Ryan didn't notice that Gabby had vanished. She'd transformed into a giant! She walked towards Ryan. It was like Gabby was brainwashed; she knew nothing about Ryan.
It all started when Ryan was in the tent this afternoon. Gabby was with him and she went out to explore. Then all of a sudden, she vanished and didn't remember anything! It was Ryan's last time to say goodbye, but he couldn't...

Abdur-Rahman Bin-Umar (9)

Waffle's Whittle Wood Adventure

Waffle the wolf was a bright little fellow. His very wise and caring grandfather had sadly passed away. He'd once told Waffle about this wondrous place in the deep, dark woods. Nobody in his family dared to enter the woods, it was forbidden to go. However, his brave, curious grandfather had ventured into the forbidden woods where he found the most magical place. He told Waffle amazing, extraordinary stories about the Whittle Woods. Waffle was given some of his grandfather's old belongings and he was astounded to find a map of the Whittle Woods and how to get there!

Ezekiel Ratcliffe (8)

Golden-Blooded

I arrived at the secret meeting place. Nobody was there. Surely, the meeting hadn't ended? I checked my watch. Suddenly, a cold hand grabbed me and yanked me into a bag.

Seconds later, I was tipped out. There were my friends. On the floor. Dead. Their wounds were oozing golden blood. I turned and saw a woman with bloodstained lips and gnarled hands that looked like they'd been carved from wood. She threw the knife she was holding. I dodged, but it skimmed my finger. Golden blood poured out. I stared momentarily, then ran through the woods, not looking back...

Sophia Dix (10)

Kind Hearts

"There has to be a way out of these woods," said Mihu, trying to sound hopeful. She and her brother had planned a picnic but now they were lost.
"I want to go home," Manu cried.
Just then, a robin appeared. Mihu's mind whizzed! She had seen this robin before! Every day, she left little bits of bread out for it. The robin was following them and knew they were lost. Strangely, the robin appeared to signal to them to follow it. Soon, they found themselves back at home - happy and with a new friend.
Moral: Kindness never goes unnoticed.

Nyra Kurvakat (8)

Glittering Woods

Suddenly, I fell into a sinkhole. It was dark and deep. I took out my torch. It looked like a grand chamber. Walls had pictures of Egyptian gods, there was gold jewellery, chariots and mummies. It looked like a pharaoh's burial chamber. Walls were covered with carvings and paintings. I heard water gushing beneath the chamber. There was a cool wind howling. Suddenly, I felt dizzy.

When I woke up, the sun was shining on my face. My mother was shouting, "Wake up!" Realising all of this was a dream, with a heavy heart, I started getting dressed for school.

Atharva Tyagi (9)

The Eerie Forest

Today, I had a walk in the forest. Not a pleasant walk, a scary walk. Walking around, I heard the deafening sound of an abundance of creatures. A different variety of wolves howled and sounded weary. The thunderous growls of bears who were enraged about hibernation ending now that it was a fresh, new season. I noticed the trees. Some blossom trees had begun to bloom like a lovely flower. However, most had stayed withered after the astonishing coldness of a peculiar winter where snow fell like torrential rain.
Still, the forest had me enchanted as I watched in awe.

Maheshwari Kumar (10)

What A Fright!

I'd escaped from my wicked stepmother and wandered through the gloomy woods. All of a sudden, I heard an unusual sound. There stood a campfire. Next to it were two white figures talking. I was confused, so I hid behind a blackberry bush, then peered through the vines and overheard them saying, "Within these woods, lies a furious beast that only comes out of its dark, creepy cave at midnight hunting for its prey. It's allergic to ghosts, so we're lucky."

After I heard that, I ran back home and hid under my cosy blanket and shivered anxiously.

Aiza Anwaar (8)

The Enchanted Forest

Once upon a time, there lived two girls Jenna and Sabrina. They both wanted to go to the woods. One night, they sneaked out. They were only nine and twelve. They walked and walked until they reached the woods. They saw a brown and white fox running and muttering to himself. They reached the fox and asked, "Do you know where we are?"

"Yes I do!" explained the fox. "I will help you." They reached the door. They went through the door and saw loads of candy. They saw water horses and fire horses, ice horses and finally wind horses.

Aiza Arfan

The Enchanted Woods

Darkness was drawing in and Lilly and her family were having a walk in the nearby woods. Suddenly, the trees turned golden. Mum and Dad were so stunned by the beauty of the forest they didn't notice Lilly wander off on her own adventure.
Lilly strode off next to a flowing stream. Slipping, she fell into the cool water, blue in colour with beautiful swans gliding by. Flow, the darkest and most elegant swan, was gliding slowly and carried Lilly back to her amazed parents, tucked under her feathers. They thanked Flow and they returned gratefully to their home.

Ruqaiya-Imaan Alam (9)

The Wild Horse In The Woods

Shannon and Mark had a trail from their garden to the woods. They went for a walk there every day. One sunny day, they saw something running through the woods. They came closer and saw it was actually a wild horse! Suddenly, they realised there were horse thieves in the distance trying to get the horse into their truck. They bolted over and attacked them. *Thud!* The thieves fell to the floor. "Yay!" they shouted loudly. They had managed to save the horse. They took the horse to their garden and decided they would keep him. They named him Wild.

Archie Holliday (9)

A Wander In The Woods

Strolling through the forest, burnt orange, amber and muddy brown surround me like a blanket. With one foot in front of the other, a gentle autumn breeze touches my fingertips and dead leaves rustle under my feet in the background. Chestnut squirrels leap from branch to branch and colourful birds all nestle together in a small, happy community. Ancient trees tower over me like skyscrapers, stretching to reach the white, fluffy clouds as they lazily lay above me. The air is thick and dense. I look up to the endless turquoise sky and take a deep breath. I feel better.

Sohalia Sarkar

A Fox's Tale

My puppies were born in the depths of my beloved valley. Days passed as I watched them grow curious and ambitious. As winter drew closer, food became scarce. It was time to leave what had been our haven for several months. We set forth into the unknown wilderness.

As we strolled through the birch forest, our paws grew stiff and we yearned for water. As we got nearer to our destination, a huntsman's horn brewed eerily on the breeze. Suddenly, I sensed the motion of hooves heading our way. Quickly, we scrambled into a burrow as horses leapt overhead. Safe...

Esme Richardson (10)

The Wolf

It was getting dark as the winter sun began to fall, casting hauntingly long shadows through the woodland. Snowy clouds puffed from my lips as my peaceful wander turned into a frantic run; heart thundering, lungs panting. Panting, thundering, the wolf was coming! The icy January moon arced across the sky. Racing towards a gnarly oak, I hauled myself upwards through the thick branches. The wolf appeared in the clearing below, circling, lifting its head to the moon. Our eyes met as a single drop of drool hung from its jowls. The wolf howled at the wolf moon hungrily.

Caitlin Butterfield

The Season Forest

Once, there was a fairy princess who invited her friends to a picnic in the season forest.

They happily went to the forest. They saw a blossom tree. "It's really pretty," said the fairy princess. Then the sun started getting hot, so they took off their outer clothes and jumped into the lake and splashed around! But then the wind started howling and blew them down the steep waterfall in a gust of brown leaves!

Wonderfully the water froze and they flew right out of it. They put on some warm clothes and started ice skating, having lots of fun!

Anna Leigh Okafor-Withers (8)

Lost In The Woods

It was getting dark as Kat entered the enchanted forest, she smelt the damp tree bark. Kat turned on her torch but a few seconds later it began flickering. She heard the trees creaking as they swayed. Kat began shaking as she realised she was lost! While frantically searching for her way back, a werewolf howled! Immediately, Kat hid under a rotting log but she felt something tickling her back, it was a huge spider! She ran out, shrieking. Kat heard her mum shouting her name. They ran towards one another in disbelief. Shivering, they carefully made their way home.

Maja Wnuk (11)

The Speaking Tree

In pursuit of folklore tales of the speaking tree, something stopped me. I felt a shiver slither down my spine. A dark, skeletal figure was lurking deep within the shadows. Its fingers unravelled from behind a colossal tree. Past several trees, it raced. I took a stride and leapt off the ground, following intently.

Seconds later, it stopped and mysteriously vanished. I retraced its steps, wary of my surroundings and soon discovered a tree looming in the blinding sunlight. Not any ordinary tree, but one with a face, a mouth and a voice. The speaking tree...

Yahya Abrar

A Wander In The Woods

I'd escaped from the enchanted castle, running as fast as my legs could carry me. Suddenly, I stumbled over some tree roots and I was looking at a world of lollipops. Not exactly my dreamland. Suddenly, I saw my deceased brother and he was staring right at me! We jumped over candyfloss clouds, but we misstepped and we were back at the enchanted castle. The overflowing pot of frog gruel slithered towards us. There were manky cobwebs spouting dust and jars of frogs' eyes and cats' tails. I decided to escape again, but then something pulled me down...

Thaaniya Nandakumar (11)

Mission Fairy

"Maybe we could have a fairy exhibit?" I said to the museum manager excitedly.

"Nonsense!" he shouted.

"Fairies are real! I'll prove it!" I argued as I left the room.

I went to the woods: Mission Fairy. I kept walking, walking and walking but then my torch ran out of battery! If I didn't find light soon, night would come and I would be lost! I looked for a while in the dark, misty woods and I noticed something shimmering and glowing in a tree trunk. I went closer, and to my surprise, there it was... proof; a fairy fossil.

Zenia Moghal (8)

One Day In The Woods

Today, it was warm and sunny, so me and Mum went for walk. I thought this day was going to go well... In the distance, I heard a howl. "Mum, there's a wolf!" I screamed.
"Don't be so silly!" said Mum, laughing, "Just enjoy the birds singing and all the pretty flowers." I was terrified. I wanted to run home but I couldn't leave Mum with the wolves! Then I heard Mum yell like never before. I swiftly sprinted towards her, faster than ever before. She was fine, there was no wolf. If it wasn't there, where was it?

Ava Swift (9)

The Fearful Wait By The Fire

It was getting dark. The flicker of the campfire reflected in my emerald green eyes. The orange and red leaves on the dying trees rustled as the wind pierced my skin. I was as cold as the heart of the most despicable man. My brown, rain-soaked hair sagged down my back. I was starting to think he wouldn't show up. Then I heard the crunching of leaves and sticks behind me. "You thought I wouldn't show up, didn't you?" said a deep, chilling voice out of sight.

I jumped up from my bed sweating and whimpering. The nightmare had returned.

Eleanor Harp (10)

The Monster In The Forest

I ran as fast as I could, heart beating, air tearing through my lungs, legs begging to stop. Lightning struck a large oak, cutting the grey abyss of clouds that hung over the forest. Rain hammered down, making the ground wet and boggy, intensifying the smell of rotting leaves and smouldering wood. The two-headed, spiky, brown-haired monster was getting closer. The faster I ran, the more dehydrated I got. My lips were so dry, they were stuck to my teeth. The monster roared and was as fast as an athlete in a race. He jumped up and grabbed me. "Arghh!"

Gabriel Wittrock (10)

The Mystical Forest!

There must be a way out. I have to continue, no matter what happens. As I went through the pitch-black forest, I saw colossal trees hovering above me. It gave me a spine-chilling sensation. Irritating insects started to crawl on me which made the hairs on my arms stand up. With anxiety and nervousness, I continued the journey to find my lost daughter. Then suddenly, I found something that was beyond my wildest imagination. A portal! It was a big, glimmering circle that was as bright as the sun. Did my daughter possibly go in there? I decided to go...

Asmitha Thayaruban (10)

Unicorn Mystery

Once there was an elven queen who wanted to steal something. What, though? Everyone thought she was pretty because she gave the greatest presents.

But one day, a little unicorn came. She tiptoed. *Trit-trot*, she went. The queen came out of her palace, but the unicorn was not there. Why?

The next day, the queen came out of her palace again and saw a white thing. It was the unicorn. The queen fainted because unicorns are not real. But they became friends in the forest. Now they are happy. They take rides in the forest. Everyone is happy.

Grace Navi (7)

The Time-Worn Man

In a distance from the great tree were squirrels climbing up and down. There were falling damp leaves and dancing branches. The wind blew the leaves which exposed a small door. The door had a zigzag design and an ancient gold knocker. It was silent for once. The door looked abandoned. It began to open. "Who are you?" said a quiet voice. Taking a deep breath I stepped forwards taking a small peek. Inside the door was dark. I stepped inside shaking, there was the time-worn man. I'd never seen him. I took a step back hoping nothing would happen...

Leticia Ghenu

Ben And Molly In The Woods

Once upon a time, there was a boy and girl called Molly and Ben.

One day, they went into the woods. They got there and heard a crackling noise.

"Watch out!" shouted Molly. There was a monster in the woods!

"Run, Ben!" Molly shouted. The monster chased them. The monster looked very spiky. Its claws and teeth were as big as a tree. Then they found a little cave. The monster was coming but he wasn't able to fit through the cave. There were lots of spiders and snakes. One chased them but they were able to escape back home.

Ammaar Janjua (7)

Spring Ball

I'd arrived at the secret meeting place in the woods. It was getting creepy, so I tiptoed to a bush and hid behind it. From the darkness, a shadowy figure emerged. A swarm of pixies chattering like bees pulled me into a rabbit hole. Beneath the ground, I was at the annual spring ball! The pixies wore daffodil dresses and their hair sparkled like snow. We partied all night, ate acorn sandwiches and pollen pudding until it was home time. The queen blessed me with a spring promise.
As I re-entered the wood, it had transformed into a spring wonderland.

Iris Hudson (9)

An Underground Forest Below

I heard a noise behind me. A strange creature popped out of the fire. It began to fade. Two monsters appeared. A portal dragged me to a mystical place called the Forest of Banishment. I wandered around and saw a venomous tiger. Then I saw a young electric deer, a bright snake and a spider. I chose the electric deer because it would give the tiger an electric shock.

Twenty minutes later, another monster appeared: an electric snake. Then I saw three objects: battery, ruler and mirror. I chose the battery. It would zap it back. I'd completed my quest!

Muhammad Faheel Saqib (8)

The Mythoworld

In a strange, magical land mythical creatures only lived and it was called The Mythoworld. There were pixies and gryphons and trolls and dragons. There was a servant of the great lord and the servant's name was Dawn. The lord sent him on a quest to retrieve the Eye of Bliss. Dawn started his quest. He passed all the lands and the gryphons came with Dawn. An old wizard gave a riddle. "What's mightier than steel yet dies in sun?"
The servant thought about it... "Ice!" Dawn yelled. He would find the eye in an ice castle.

Dhruv Shah

The Moon Tiger

In the forest lives an ancient creature called the Moon Tiger. The Moon Tiger is a huge, blue tiger with bright green stripes. Its tail is a long, hissing, green snake and it only comes out at night which is why you should never go into the woods when it's dark.

One night, two girls did just that. *Roar!* A horrible roar came from nowhere. *Roar!* It happened again, but louder. The girls ran as fast as they could, hoping they weren't being chased. They were, by the huge, ferocious Moon Tiger! What would happen to the poor girls?

Mya Burridge (10)

Five Spylets

I heard a noise behind me. My heart began beating rapidly! It was a dark and gloomy night. The sad-looking lark had gone, all was silent. I knew the secret meeting place was close now. Big chunks of snow were at my feet making a crunching noise. I arrived, my signal was up. The campfire was lit, Skye, my friend, had talked through the plan! Agent Halo, Skye's mother, had found the PIN code. Suddenly, I began to feel brave. Alex arrived, Skye and Agent Halo searched the area. The first spylet ran to the diamond room. Footsteps crept. "Arghh!"

Navika Malhi

Curious, Creepy And Cursed

We went for a wander in the woods. It was Lauren who thought of having a wander first. Eventually, Lola and I agreed to go. We strolled casually from our class camp. We arrived in the thick of the forest where we discovered three jewels with an eerie glow illuminating them. Lola stretched her hand out daringly, but before we could snatch her hand away, something supernatural occurred from what seemed like a normal gem.

Instantly, Lola was paralysed, her limbs stiff. She fell onto the ground. If this was awful, things were about to get a lot worse...

Aaila Bint-Asif (10)

The Apple Trees

Once there was a rosy apple. She hung on a tree in the beautiful orchard waiting patiently, hoping not to be picked. On the tree opposite, hung a glistening green apple.

One day, they both got picked and chopped up. However, their seeds were saved.

The next day, there was a ray of metallic sunshine shooting through the window onto the table where the seeds sat watching. That day, the small, black apple seeds got planted. Eventually, the seeds grew into towering trees! They fell in love and started a new life together and lived happily forever.

Safiya Parsons

The Brave Elf

Once upon a time, in the Forest of Damesh, shrouded in a thick blanket of mist that kept out the nightmarish creatures that lurked in the shadows, there was a tiny, brave elf.

As he strolled through the woods, he found a gnarled, crooked door lying on the bark of a gargantuan tree. Without hesitation, he bolted through the door and found an old watch. As fast as lightning, the watch started to glow bright blue and surges of energy flowed into its old body. Instantly, he was transported to the Kingdom of Elves and reunited with his long-lost family.

Zain Ahmed (10)

The Escape

I'd had enough. This was the final straw. Mum had forced me to go to summer camp again. She was acting like she was the boss. The approach to the cabin was unpleasant and the sleeping area worse than I had expected. I had to escape - I couldn't survive this. I hated being bossed around.
I ventured into the forest when no one was looking. The wind was howling ferociously. The forest was filled with vines circling the trees like snakes and blanketing the woods with darkness. Then suddenly, out of nowhere, a tiger launched out of the bush...

Asha Webster (10)

Squirrel In The Woods

Behind me, I heard a *tap-tap-tapping*. There, sitting peacefully in a large oak tree, I saw a squirrel cracking a nut. I wandered closer. The bright red squirrel abruptly jerked its head to one side and stared at me curiously. I smiled. If there was anything that made me happy, it was seeing nature in its natural habitat. I ambled closer still... I knew not to make any sudden movements that would scare him. *Snap!* A twig cracked underneath me. The squirrel hurried to one side and disappeared. The big, fluffy bundle was gone... for now.

Rebecca Morrison (8)

The Haunted Door

As I was walking in the decaying woods, I stumbled across an ancient door. How strange! A sign announced: 'Do not open!' Old hinges and a rusting handle called me forward to open the door, never one to do as I was told. With a deafening creak, the door opened slowly. As I peeked inside, an invisible hand dragged me through. Once through, I could feel shivers running up and down my spine. Whispers terminated from the flourishing oak trees. A curious mist around my feet. A feeling of being targeted came over me. It had begun... my unwilling end.

Kayla Culley

The Huge Rocket

Once, there was a little boy called Maryou. He was eight and he loved building stuff.

One day, he made a huge rocket using a cardboard box, buttons, tin foil, a handlebar, plastic and bottles. It took one hour to plan and nine hours to build.

When it was bedtime, the rocket turned on and Maryou woke up and jumped into the rocket. He flew to the moon and met a nice alien. They had so much fun jumping and doing backflips. Then Maryou travelled home.

The next morning, his mum said, "Close the window, please. It's very cold!"

Guillem Bonet (6)

The Lost Puppy

Once, a tiny puppy curled up in fear as the whole wood shook at a scary pace. *I must save my children*, she thought. "There's no wind," she said worriedly. The truth was: she was lost. She was wishing that her owner would come when suddenly, she heard her name being called out. "Joy, come here!" Joy was confused but she was so scared, she kept on running. Joy kept hearing her name, so she looked in the bush and she found her owner! "Oh, Joy, come here! Come on, let's go home. Thank goodness, I found you."

Matilda Anthopoulos (8)

Wander In The Woods

Trees swayed to the rhythm of the wind and birds chirping brought the forest harmony alongside the still breeze. Moving forward, a sudden sound caught my ears - looking carefully, I saw something like a million crystals gushing as the golden rays of the sun abandoned them into obliteration. Underneath my feet, laid out, was a carpet of a billion colours, colours that no one could ever even think of - the colours of nature! Staring above me, I watched as the golden sphere slowly made its way down, sinking into the big blue patch which was now black...

Kinza Naveed

The Ghost

Do you believe in ghosts? A boy called Bob does... because he saw one. One day, Bob and Jeff were walking through the sunny woods with Bob's dog. Suddenly, the wood went as murky as night. Downpour. Bob's dog started barking. They saw a white figure. A ghost. It wandered away from them. Suddenly, they heard a noise from behind them. It was just Bob's dog. Then... Bob suddenly saw the ghost again. He sprinted away. The ghost was almost in front of them. Bob made it to safety, Jeff didn't. Bob was the lucky one, Jeff was definitely not.

Gabriel Spencer-Bird

A Gigantic Sandcastle

One sunny day, Maya was on the beach playing in the sand. She decided to make a sandcastle. So she called her friends and they all started searching for decorations for the sandcastle. They found seashells and seaweed. Then they started to make a gigantic sandcastle that was big enough for them to fit in.

When they were almost finished, their mums came to see what they were doing. They were proud when they saw what their children were doing. When they had finished, they started to play in the sandcastle. After that, it was time to go home.

Khadija Adams (8)

A World Of Fantasy

She had been walking happily in the woods.
A while later, she entered the secret rings. She
wondered what was in these mysterious rings, so
took her first step. As this girl with sapphire eyes, a
flowery headband and rainbow hair stepped in,
she was awestruck. She saw a mystical place and
it was a world of fantasy. It was glorious and truly
outstanding. Then she spotted a cloud and climbed
up to it to explore further. Shivers went down her
spine. She faced her fears and went into the dingy,
smoky forest. With a sprinkle of dust, she
vanished...

Umika Singh (8)

The Nightcaller

Faster than an arrow, James raced through the prehistoric woods, not looking where he was going. All he knew was that he had to get away from it. He sprinted past a cluster of trees that disappeared at first glance. In the far distance was a tall, rugged cliff. Dread slipped down James' throat; how would he get out of this one? He had to think quick, the Nightcaller was coming. A growl from the distance signalled James to move faster. Above him, was a tree longer and more ancient than the others. Already, James was climbing, higher and higher...

Inaya Javed (10)

The Hidden Door

As eerie darkness descended on the eerie wood, I painstakingly trudged through the sticky mud. My feet sank with each step I took. As I walked on, I pushed away the abundance of gnarled branches. Jagged rocks stood out of the ground and I tripped. My face slipped across the squelchy mud and I tumbled down a coarse slope. In front, stood an old oak tree and a door with the carved out number: 666. I rose and carefully opened the door slowly, cautiously. I excitedly stepped inside... As I entered the door slammed behind me and I was trapped...

Kiya Bhatt (10)

Woods

I'm huddled around a campfire as the sky grows dark, alone and abandoned by my so-called friends. I feel spiders climbing my spine. I feel these woods are enchanted as I hear quiet whispers of the forest around me. I decide to start settling down for the night. As I blow at the campfire, everything turns black. Suddenly, I hear a small rustle coming from the bushes. Intrigued, I slowly stumble towards them, holding a stick as my only defence. I pull back the bushes and trip, then feel myself fall into what seems like a dark hole of eternity...

Emilia Pennie (10)

A Dark Wood

It was a dark night in the woods and everything was surrounded by murky shadows. A teenage boy named Ben knew that this wood had been full of epoch events. However, he valiantly approached the abandoned cottage and stepped inside. The dark shadows of the loft didn't frighten him and he investigated his surroundings thoroughly, looking for clues to see if someone once lived there.

To his horror, he saw that the door was open, even though he had shut it already. He was not alone. He sprinted outside and saw there was a ghost approaching...

Sulaimaan Mohammed (10)

A Wander In The Woods

Snap! Went the twigs underneath my feet. I was following a butterfly - continually dragging a stick in the mud. This way, I knew I wouldn't get lost. I had no idea where this butterfly was taking me, but I was getting closer to something; I couldn't see what it was yet. My mouth dropped open and the stick fell from my grasp as I looked up at the ancient building in front of me. The building was covered in vines and crumbling before me. The butterfly flew away, but that didn't bother me. Ahead of me was an undiscovered castle.

Elysia Barno (10)

A Fairy In A Land Of Wonder

In a land of fairies, the purple sky shone in a dark forest with twigs snapping, leaves rustling, waterfalls shining in the purple sunset. *Bang!* A new fairy came to the forest for a whole month, in the land of wonder. Fairy two, named Lily, and fairy one, named Adiya, walked and walked. *Whoosh!* A magical book appeared in Adiya's hand. She started to read the book about purple wings that can glow in the night. A goblin came into the woods with an axe. Luckily, they were back in the sky with fluffy clouds, dancing on the moon.

Chantelle Nakintu Mwanje

Emily And The Woodland Ghost

It was getting dark when Emily found the tree that had the strange symbol. Four intricately carved lines, shaped like veins in a hand, merged together into a spiral. Emily ran her hands along the design, it was special no doubt. She was about to touch the tree again when an ugly man appeared to walk out of the tree. His hands were bony, his fingers were gnarled and the side of his face was covered in blood. Emily gaped, shocked. "Are you trying to catch flies?" asked the man, amused. "If you touch my tree, you die."
She fled.

Sayali Joglekar (11)

The Crystal

It started 100 years ago, parts of the Crystal of Power were in danger. The Guardians of the Clans put their part of the crystal on the Thinking Stone and a portal appeared. The crystal parts joined and the portal sucked it in.

100 years later, the descendants of the clans that lived in the magical forest, were in their temple wondering where the crystal was. A portal appeared and they got sucked in. They came to an agreement with the others. The crystal separated. Each clan got their piece of the crystal and the portal took them back home.

Keira Brown

The Attack In The Ferocious Forest

As lion-hearted Leo was zooming on his motorbike, he gazed lovesick at the nature. After some time, he came to a wall. To anyone else, this wall might've seemed like just a slab of stone, but not to Leo. He scraped away some dust with his gloves, only to find a big 'H' encrusted into the stone. Curiously, he pressed it. A huge castle made of trees appeared behind the rock. Suddenly, a monster that was no more than 50ft tall arose. He grabbed a bloodstained sword from a high shelf and stood poised in the position of murder...

Ali Nagey (9)

My Magical Encounters

I was walking silently through the path of the forest. Suddenly, I was transported to a different world! It was amazing. Then I realised something, I was flying! Was I a fairy? To confirm my theory, I tried to summon a magic wand and to my amazement, it worked! I looked around me. I saw munchkins, fairies, snow sprites and golden eagles.
I flew up to a fairy and asked, "Where am I?"
She replied, "In the fairy world."
She offered me a sweet and I was going to eat it...
My alarm rang. I wish I was there again...

Heritage Agbaje (9)

The Whispering Woods

Today was a very miserable day. As the clouds were weeping, the cheerful flowers hung their heads low and everybody was so slow. There was one girl, Kristy, who hung her head high through all the rough times. She wasn't like anyone else. She asked her parents if she could visit the woods to clear her head. It was nearly teatime.

As she strolled down the path, she sang a lovely tune to help the flowers bloom. She suddenly heard a voice whispering quietly through the trees. With fear, she went home. She was hoping to go back next year...

Manreet Kaur (10)

From A Stroll In The Woods... To Planet Leron

Andy was taking a stroll away from her horrible parents. She didn't go to school. Andy was really upset. Suddenly, her foot slipped. There were people. They were pink. She was on a different planet! She suddenly realised she was interrupting a fight. She then realised she could somehow help them. So she stood up and put the two chiefs' hands together and they realised they were wrong to fight. She stayed there for a few months. The name of the planet was Leron. She then decided to live with the tribespeople and lived happily ever after.

Sofia McMillan (8)

A Journey Through The Woods

I arrived at the secret meeting place. I thought my friend would be waiting for me next to the cave near the woods, but no. *Maybe she's in the woods*, I said to myself. So I went into the woods. Immense trees were welcoming me. The ground was rutted and muddy in some places. I was looking around the woods and suddenly, a fierce, strong tiger roared at me. *Roar, roar, roar!* I was petrified. Then the petrifying tiger ran away into the darkness. I was confused. I texted my friend and asked: 'Where are you?' No reply...

Dhieshaa Sureshkumar (8)

Trapped

The light was dimming as the sun glided past the horizon. Up and down Britain, people were slipping into a calm slumber. Not me. Neither were the elves! My heart was beating hard. I could feel it pounding with every breath I took. Night was descending fast; if I didn't get home, I would perish in the cold, wintery conditions. Behind me, elves drew nearer as I stumbled through the moss and the brambles, my feet getting caught in the weeds. Up ahead, the path widened and I could see civilisation, but the village wall blocked my path. Trapped!

Lillian May Pedley (12)

The True Warrior

I arrived at the secret meeting place. Was the legend true? A man would come from the sky and fight a dragon? Suddenly, it started to thunder, a man appeared. Next, a dragon. They talked with hatred. Lava sailed around the man, a lava axe appeared, then armour. The man shouted, "Fight!" The dragon flapped its wings and started to fly around the man swiftly. Bravely he swung his axe on the dragon's leg, then the dragon started to moan. The dragon began to spit fireballs at the man, he dodged all of them. The man was a true warrior.

Tayyib Patel (9)

The Boy In The Woods

It was a nice, clear day. Max was skipping across the woods. He wasn't scared. You could say he was excited. He always wanted to taste wild fruits and watch wild plants. He longed to explore the woods. He walked a little bit more and tried a fruit. *It's so sweet*, he thought to himself.

While Max was walking, he made an amazing plan. He was going to make a magnificent treehouse and eat the delicious fruits. He wouldn't have to worry about family because he was an orphan. So he built a treehouse and lived there forever.

Amelia Szaja (10)

Following The Path Of A Stream

Waking up, unconsciously, you look down and see that you are on a small boat. You realise you have fallen asleep while fishing. What could possibly go wrong? You find yourself drifting across a small river that's pushing you towards a forest. Down you go, the water just gets clearer as the sun rises above you. You look at a variety of fish swimming below you in a shoal. It could never get more peaceful. The vibrant birds singing beautifully and the luscious green willow trees swaying swiftly across the stream. It is like a dream come true.

Tenzin Phuntsok (11)

The Camping Trip

I was packing up for the camping trip. I was only a little bit scared because we were going to a forest. Maya and Katie were ready, so I had to be really quick. I packed up and zoomed to my friends.
"Yes, we are here!" cried Maya as we arrived in the forest.
"It looks creepy," said Katie looking at the willow tree's old branches.
"Arghh!" cried Maya as loud as you can imagine. "It's a monster!"
It looked like a furball. It had a tail just like a lion and ears like a rabbit...

Anabia Javed (8)

The Door

The woods were quiet, peaceful for that matter.
Yet something felt wrong. Maisy and her dog kept
moving forward. All of a sudden, there was a
massive clearing. But still, Maisy carried on moving
and her eyes feasted on something else. A door.
Yep, that's right. A door. This door wasn't like any
ordinary door though. This door wasn't an opening
into a building or a room. Just a door and a door
frame. She found it quite cute and intriguing, so
she decided to walk through it. What happened
next, she was not ready, nor prepared for...

Scarlett Dowkes (9)

Camping Lock-In

It was getting towards night-time as the sky turned into a mass of fiery shades. Burning balls of light hung in the pitch-black sky, illuminating the crescent moon. I set up a campfire in an abandoned, mossy cave with dry logs and heard the wind howl outside, making the flames flicker. Just as I was about to go out, the rocky wall rumbled, then caved in, trapping me. Shadows loomed and bounced off the walls of the cave and the occasional snaps of twigs breaking could be heard. *There must be a way out!* I thought, dreading the outcome.

Jasmine Davies (10)

Locked In Her Own Fears

In the distance, I saw something minuscule and glittery. I edged a little closer to see a gorgeous bluebell, except this bluebell was frozen. But how? The scorching sun was seeping through the tall, towering trees. *How strange*, I thought, but I still hurried along a winding serpentine path. I froze and let my curiosity get the better of me as I pulled a curtain of seaweed slightly ajar. Suddenly, I felt as if I was drowning in sadness. Terrible thoughts hit me. I was then abruptly kneeling by a deathbed, but whose? I leant closer...

Diya Jain (10)

A Deathly Mistake

The moon had driven the sun out of the sky and the solitary darkness had swept across the woodland, followed by the vicious, icy draught. That was when I first heard it. A mournful squeak. Countless times before, I had come to these deserted woods but I had never heard anything like it. The sound came again. This time louder, lost, more longing. Kneeling down by the fire, I crept towards it. The strong smell of rusty blood filled the air around me. I began to feel unnaturally perturbed. Then as I was taking another step forwards, I saw it...

Namyaa Singhal (10)

A Wish Regretted

There were twins who longed for adventure. Soon, they got just that. When night turned to day, they were not in their house. In the middle of the woods was their location. Witches, vampires and goblins surrounded them like in the tales they'd heard. They were now separated, one on either side of the villains. Were they really just thinking about the pros but not the cons to their wish? Now they had to choose which villain amongst them was not a villain but a hero that'd get them home. If they succeeded or not, we shall never know...

Anaiah Da Cunha (10)

The Scary Woods

Once upon a time, Jimmy went camping with his parents who went looking for firewood. They'd been gone for ages. He had no phone, it was dark and cold, and Jimmy was scared. He went to find help but the campsite was deserted. He felt like he was the only person in the world.

Whilst walking bravely along in the shadows, he found an old pub. He went inside, finding food, drink and a roaring fire, but strangely, still nobody around. He ate, drank and warmed up before falling asleep, only to be woken by the door slowly creaking open...

Jonathan Miller (8)

A Magical Mission

I arrived at the secret meeting place where a wizard was telling everyone their missions. My mission was to go to a magical valley. A guard appeared to try and stop me from completing my mission. I defeated the guard and went through the golden gates. The place looked mysterious and ancient. I was surprised to find natural artefacts. I had to solve a riddle before I could pick anything up. If I didn't, the gates would shut, I would trip the alarm and the building would collapse. Thankfully, I solved the riddle and grabbed a few pieces.

Nicole Abitimo Oloya (8)

Colossal Camp Surprise

One chilly, winter morning, Lora and her family were trudging quietly in the dark woods. It was Lora's first time camping due to her young age. It took her hours to set up camp and at last, they sat back to admire their work.

That night, through the hooting of an owl visible in a ray of moonlight, a different sound filled the sky. Moments later, Lora was out of bed and creeping towards the sound. Suddenly, she laid eyes on a silver-horned deer lying near a hard rock. Lora gasped. This was the best holiday she'd ever had.

Likya Meis Bultan (8)

Run!

Blood pounds through my veins, leaves crunch behind me, I must keep on running. Howls of the wolves behind me echo in the misty, musty, forest. My leg bangs against a sharp rock, it's bleeding! Taking my chance, I scramble up the nearest tree just missing wolves. Even though I can't see them, I know they're there, waiting, watching for me to come down, ripping a piece of my cloak, I tie it around my leg. I can hear howling and the snapping of the wolves as they begin to leave. Perfect silence, then the tree begins to rumble...

Chinmayi Reghunath

A Wander In The Woods

It was getting dark as Sammy the squirrel overheard goblins whispering about an evil plan to destroy the magical statue.
The next day, Sammy sat thinking about the goblins and made up a plan to stop them.
That night, along with two friends, he set off to find the goblins. They found them and followed them to a cave where the magical statue was.
As they entered, they saw the huge, ancient statue in the centre. As quick as a flash, they caught hold of the goblins with a rope, before happily taking them to the police station.

Sophie Bellwood (9)

The Witch In The Woods

Once upon a time, deep in the woods lived an evil witch called Ryzak. At the bottom of the woods was a village where a community of people lived with their children. All the villagers were aware of the witch, Ryzak, and warned their children about her and told them not to go into the woods.

One day, a group of five unlucky kids decided to skip school and instead have a wander in the woods to pass the time. Suddenly, they stumbled across the witch's cottage and were seized by Ryzak's evil spell. They were never seen again...

Mariam Imran

The Dark Woods

I moved towards the dark, daring woods. It was a terrible idea! I could only see close by because of the fogginess. The trees were dead, standing still. As I walked deeper into the intimidating woods, I was getting more and more terrified. There were skeleton hands sticking out of the tall, thick trees. Soon, I could only see dead people on the floor. Then I realised I was trapped in a circle of skeletons and fearful creatures. The trees whooshed towards me, making the circle that I was in smaller and smaller. I fell down to the ground!

Luis Gjoka (10)

Deep In The Forest

It's cold, quiet and dark. I've been locked in here for three days now, somewhere deep in the forest. It all began on my usual forest trail walk on Saturday. I'd been walking for about 40 minutes when I heard a peculiar clamour. It sounded like a screech. Without hesitation, I went over to check it out, but that's when I knew all wasn't right. I saw a strange being lying on the leaves, face down.
Just then, someone knocked me out. I woke up in some sort of dingy hut. Why have they done this? How will I escape?

James Morrissey (10)

A Lively Day In The Woods

As I enter the forest, I smell something funny. Is it some sticky tree sap or some sweet honey from a lively beehive? Oh... it's just horse dung! *I knew I should have worn Wellington boots!* I tell myself as I drag my feet through the disgusting, squishy, icky mud with my red, now very brown, trainers. I moan to my dad, "Are we there yet?" But he just won't respond.

After more than an hour, I am curious how much longer is left to walk when finally, I see the black car that we arrived in, in the distance!

Trisha Varkey (9)

The Melting Of The Earth

In the distance, we saw Earth melting! So we zoomed back to Earth in our spectacular spaceship. Everyone was panicking when we got there. There was a mysterious cackling to be heard from the sky. We followed the noise and reached a solid wall that said: *'Beware'* on it. So we said in Parseltongue, "Beware." It cleared and we saw an evil sorcerer who was cackling. We tied him in ropes and threw him into the core of the Earth. Then he was dead! Everyone was so happy and we were famous! It was the best day ever!

Emily Silver (8)

The Dragon

The howling wind billowed in front of me as the dangerous dragon reared its giant wings. The trees were the only things separating us from each other. Breathing red-hot fire, the dragon burnt them down. All I needed was my hoverboard, so I tapped on the screen of my smartwatch which had unfortunately run out of battery. It died when I really needed it the most! But what was that red glint in the sky? My hoverboard! I gasped, lunging forward, but the dragon was too quick. My stomach dropped. My only hope was gone now. What would I do?

Aryan Yadav (11)

A Night Out

Alan heard footsteps coming nearby. He could clearly hear the crunching of snow. He knew that something was trying to locate him. He had to hide but luckily, that wasn't a hard thing to do in the forest at night. Out of the left corner of his eye, he saw a massive tree where many smaller trees intertwined. *How convenient*, he thought while crouching down behind it. He saw a man who was snooping around with a gun in his hand. A hunter? Alan did not want to be the prey. How could he escape the threatening danger before him?

Aarush Ram

Who's There?

She was hearing voices in her head... again.
Earlier that year, the wind whistled in Lucy's ears
as she walked down the narrow path in the woods.
It was a dreary day and she was drenched to the
skin. Lucy was camping with her family but she
was bored, so she had wandered into the forest to
search for something interesting - she hadn't
found anything. Turning around to head back, she
heard a voice. Her eyes widened. "Who's there?"
She couldn't make out what the voice was saying.
It was deep and gruff...

Ishba Huq

A Wander In The Woods

It was a dark and stormy night. We were camping on a moonlit field, deep in the woods. No one could enjoy their warm, cosy sleep because rain and hail thundered down on the tent spookily. We all huddled together until suddenly, we heard a howl right next to us! We all screamed at the top of our lungs, rushed out of the tent and scuttled into the trees to get away! We kept running and stumbling until we reached a clearing that was magical but gloomy. Standing in the mist, petrified, a twig snapped. Our adventure was just beginning...

Sophia Simmons

Peculiar Looking...?

Wandering in the mist of the dark, eerie woods, staggering on something abnormally thorny, long and pointed, I suspected it would just be some sort of spur. I told myself to leave it and be on my way, yet my curiosity got the better of me, before I knew it, I'd reached down to inspect the object, which I had at the time thought harmless. To my shock, it was not a spur, not a regular stone, as I had thought it'd be. I found myself clutching what appeared to be a claw, sharp and peculiar-looking. This definitely meant trouble.

Dua Umer (11)

Ash And The Majestic Deer

There was a boy named Ash who wandered through the woods searching for the majestic deer. Legend had it, it could grant any wish.

As Ash searched the woods, he found a herd of deer. He heard voices. It was the deer speaking to him! Ash was amazed, so he followed the deer. They led him to the one and only majestic deer! Ash's family were poor, so he wished for money to help his family. The deer granted it and followed Ash home to protect his family forever. Ash's family were amazed and they all lived happily ever after.

Chisomeje Emeka-Gwacham (8)

The Camping Trip

Nobody had ever found him. It all started when Max decided to go camping for his birthday. It was fun at first; they toasted marshmallows, had a laugh and told scary stories. Then they heard peculiar sounds in the distance. They looked at each other but carried on talking. Suddenly, they heard it again and this time, Leo stepped up to find out what it was.

A few hours had passed and Leo wasn't back. The friends began to worry and went looking for him for hours. He was nowhere to be found. Was he dead? Alive? Nobody knew...

Zainab Afsar (11)

Lost In The Enchanted Forest

It was getting dark. Suddenly, I heard a noise. A snarling, growling noise. Trembling, I backed off and was back-to-back with a tree. I turned and thankfully, it was a regular tree. However, I didn't know that a hidden, mysterious world was waiting for me. Unfortunately, I tripped over a tree stump and landed in a cave that was bitterly cold and very dark. I saw a light shining and I walked towards it. I stepped in the light. It felt like I was flying. I arrived and saw wonders. Magical things. It was very mystical and amazing!

Aima Saqib (10)

Haunted House

One morning, I was strolling through the forest with my friends Vinudi and Cathrine. As we went deeper into the forest, from the corner of our eyes, we saw something that was grey. It was a castle! A princess ran out screaming, "Help!" A zombie was chasing her. We suddenly realised it was allergic to water. If it was wet, all the other deadly creatures would die. We poured water on it and our plan worked! The princess and the king thanked us and gave us a sack of gold. We went home. It was the most unforgettable day ever!

Shofei Shanthakumar (8)

Lost In The Wood

Morgan had just arrived at her school residential at Green Wood. She loved adventures, but this time she was with her best friend, Jade. Suddenly, they both heard a rustle in the bushes. They kept quiet and went to investigate until... Morgan noticed that they had gone too far. They started to panic. They tripped on an odd-looking tree stump and there were only two trees, one with a glimmering pink diamond hanging from the branch with birds chirping. Jade put the gem in her pocket and tried to run. How will they ever get home now?

Liliana O'Mallo

A Wander In The Woods

In the woods, myself and my family were sharing a delicious meal. It was getting dark and gloomy so we decided to head to our tents.

During the night, I needed to get some water but all was pitch-black. After continuously walking, I stumbled upon someone that I'd never seen before! Before I made a run for it, I wasn't completely sure if it was my dad. When I asked who he was, his long, dreaded hand covered my mouth and he put me in a coal-black bag. I was petrified and had nowhere to escape. I wished my life goodbye.

Jasmine Kaur Gill (11)

The Boom!

Last night, I had the eeriest adventure of my life. As I entered the abandoned wood, I could feel the trees staring back at me like silent sentries. I could hear the sheer gusts of the wind. As I walked closer to the dilapidated woods, I looked side-to-side and saw repugnant vermin sprawling across what was once a flourishing land, abundant with animals. I looked ahead of me. I saw a little cottage adjacent to a large oak tree. I slowly opened the door. *Boom!* The whole world just disappeared. Mum and Dad had woken me up.

Pooja Koripalli (7)

My Incredible Encounter In The Woods

I was trekking through the woods when my eyes caught sight of a large stag. It had huge antlers that would clearly be victorious in battle. The stag had a strong, muscular body that would warn anyone not to mess with him. Suddenly, the earth beneath me began to shake. Through the misty woods, black silhouettes came into view and a whole herd of stags started running towards me. It was clear, this was no ordinary stag, but the leader of this herd! In a flash, I darted home through the woods to share this exciting news with my mum.

Saveen Wickramaratne (9)

Magic In The Woods

As I walked through the woods, I found a mysterious opening in the bushes. Curiosity got the better of me as I ventured in. A centaur greeted me into the unknown. I pushed open the alluring door with a pounding heart. My eyes remained wide open as I faced a fire-breathing dragon. Flying around were fairies with glistening wings. It felt like walking on a soft carpet as fallen leaves from the trees covered my path. As I approached a magnificent tree, it spoke! My heart skipped a beat. I ran as fast as the cheetah. Was this Heaven?

Aditya Bassan (7)

Wandering Into The Unknown

There once was a boy called Danny who loved adventures.

One day, he was coming home when a colossal lightning bolt hit him. He woke up confused. He saw a wood nearby and thought, *Why not go in?* Whilst Danny was walking through the woods, he suddenly felt a speck of regret. He turned around but shook it off. Danny had been on many perilous adventures but none like this one. Danny didn't know where to go, so he went straight. Would he get back home alive? Would he come back dead? Who knows, only time does...

Suveethan Sureshkumar (9)

The Woods

I didn't want to. I had to. Yes or no? Should I or shouldn't I? The questions were racing through my head. My heart was pounding. After all, the forest had claimed many victims. My parents. My aunt. My friend. I decided to go. I had all the essentials. Holding my chin up, I walked into the woods. Would I get out again? I did not know...
My eyes darted from tree to tree. There were wolves in this place, but whatever dangers there were, they were concealed by the thick trees. A waterfall up ahead. A chance for rest...

Eliza Aroush Ehjaz (9)

Lost In The Frost

I regret running off now I'm in this maze of towering trees. Pitifully, I think of what may be waiting to devour me. I shiver, not knowing if it is cold or fear. Suddenly, soft moonlight streams through a miniscule gap in the canopy onto a frost-cloaked rock. I remember that the ice will be thicker at the edge of the forest. I can see more frost sparkling on leaves as I walk tentatively forwards. I walk until the ground becomes white. I can now see the sky and the town's orange glow. I'm no longer lost and race home.

Sophie Goodwin (11)

The Treacherous Woods

I heard a twig snap behind me. My heart raced faster. All I could see was fog and the mysterious shapes of trees looming over me. The sky was ebony black. I had no choice but to run. The creature behind me sounded like a dinosaur crashing through the trees. Suddenly, the ground came hurtling towards me and I found myself on the muddy floor with the stench of decay suffocating me. Then I saw the shadow of the unknown creature rustling behind the bushes. Suddenly, it jumped out. A cute, harmless bunny. I breathed a sigh of relief.

Madison Bebb (11)

Emmie

One day, I went for an adventurous walk in the woods. I went climbing trees that hugged the clouds. I wasn't scared. Suddenly, I heard a noise. I didn't know where it came from. Then a ghost appeared. The ghost was cloudy. Then lots of sparkly glitter fell from the sky.
Out of nowhere, the glitter turned into gremlins. They were all sticky and had really sharp teeth. They were all coming closer to me. I climbed a tree and found a bow. I shot them all and the ghost disappeared. I ran back home safely and ate my tea.

Anya Joy (10)

Wolves In The Woods

It was getting dark when I was heading out of the woods. I stopped suddenly when I heard something behind me. I turned around and saw wolves in the distance. They were coming towards me. I was really scared, so I was thinking about running to the exit. Nervously, I turned around but saw more wolves guarding the exit. I started climbing a tree to hide. The wolves scratched at the tree and it broke. I fell to the ground. The wolves started licking me. I found out they weren't trying to hurt me, they just wanted to be friends.

Rebecca Maling (10)

The Wonderful Weasel

One day, I woke up from a deep slumber. I found myself walking in the deep, dark woods with green grass, beautiful butterflies, luscious leaves, enormous elephants and terrific trees. From the corner of my eye, I saw a sinister snake that was ready to attack me. As quick as a flash, I ran for my life and the venomous beast followed me. Suddenly, a weasel came out of its hole and plunged onto the snake. They had a huge brawl, but in the end, the weasel won against the ferocious beast. I was safe, thanks to the wonderful weasel.

Subhan Khalid (9)

A Wander In The Woods

In the distance, there was a strange figure wandering around in the deep, dark woods. I had a mission to successfully get back to safety with my family that were having a cosy campfire. The sticks on the ground were breaking in half as this strange creature lurked around the mysterious area. I was being as silent as possible travelling to each tree for safety.

After a while, I decided to make a run for it. I rushed back to my family and we all had a great time together. That was a crazy adventure wandering in the woods!

Sumera Arshad (11)

Nightmares In The Woods

I wandered through the gloomy woods and leapt over the thorn bushes. I was still running, running from the nightmares inside my head. I couldn't stop. I couldn't look back; he was behind me. I couldn't look back, but how would I get out of this nightmare? I needed to find the king's castle. I needed to find Merlin, the king's wizard. Merlin was the greatest wizard ever. He could make any spell; a healing spell, a reading spell and a speed spell. I loved him, he was my idol. But now I needed to find him...

Georgia Duncan

The Scarecrow In The Woods

If you went down to the woods today, there would be a scarecrow as tall as a man, sat under a golden tree with straw-like hair sat on his shoulders and a hat on top. He'd be sat on a rock no bigger than a bucket, singing all day long.

A small bird sat on his shoulder and asked, "Why are you here? You should be in the field scaring us away."

The scarecrow said, "I thought I'd have a little holiday away from you birds. I'll go back later. I'll see you bright and early tomorrow."

Emelia Hanson (10)

Annabelle

In the gloomy dark, the moon shone through the leaves that danced to the floor. Annabelle was looking for an owner because her old owner had left her in the wet forest. As the trees hunched over her she saw a girl and a boy. Then a ghost scared them away and they screamed. Annabelle was mad and sad. She went back to her abandoned little hut that she'd found in the forest. The next day, the boy and girl came back. The girl became her owner because the girl had forgotten about the ghost. She was not scared anymore.

Lola-Mai Nicholls

A Lost Flying Cat

I arrived at the secret meeting place with my friends. A flying cat had gone missing there. I looked up and down, left and right, but had no clue! I flew to China, Canada, Africa, Europe, all around the world on my magic broomstick but found nothing and returned hopelessly. Then I searched unusual places like water bottles and shoes. When I was about to give up, I heard a *miaow!* I looked up at the tree. I saw the flying cat! I got a ladder from the shed and brought the flying cat to safety. I felt very delighted.

Kashish Gupta (8)

The Astonishing Adventure

Once upon a time, there was a princess whose name was Camilla. She had a unicorn and the unicorn's name was Majesta.

One day, they both had a little trip into the woods. They had a map and the map said they had to go through a troll field, a river, over a troll bridge and to the evil queen's palace.

They got through the troll field and they were relieved, they brought some rotten blue stinky cheese. The river was really cold! The troll under the bridge was really ugly and the evil queen was really mean!

Keya Joshi

The Magic Forest

Once upon a time, there was a six-year-old girl, Peggy. Her mother asked for blueberries. She took the wrong path and got lost. She walked more until she was all tired out. Suddenly, she walked through a bush. There was a magic forest! All of the animals from the forest walked her home. Peggy, who was thankful to the animals, shared her delicious blueberry pie. They all had fun. Peggy was having the best day of her life. Then Peggy said goodbye to the new friends that she had made. Her mother snapped a photo of them all!

Gabriela Nakova (7)

Shadows

Beyond the horizon, there was a house where a gothic girl named Leah lived. One day, something caught Leah's eye, so she followed it into the woods. It was like a shadow. Leah didn't know what it was but her curiosity kept her going. Leah thought that maybe if she stopped following it, it would come to her. So she did until a little head poked out from the side of a tree. Suddenly, it stepped out. It was a puma with wings. Leah stepped closer. It bent down and she climbed on. The puma flew off to Leah's home.

Poppy Smith

The Best Sweet Shop In The World!

"Hello, Mrs Bee," I said as I walked into the sweet shop. Every Tuesday, Phoebe and I would walk home via the sweet shop Mrs Bee owned near school. It was small but extraordinary inside. Today, she gave us a new, cool sweet that would give us wings and magic powers. We practised flying in the garden, then we did a loop around the city. It was so beautiful at night from above.
By Monday, our wings had disappeared. We were so excited to go and see Mrs Bee on Tuesday to get some more of those special sweets!

Willow Silver (8)

Gangster

My fingers twisted and turned as I slithered through the woods, suffocating whatever was in my way. I sucked the life out of others, lapping the droplets greedily. Insects scuttled over me, filling me with rage that they dared to use me in this way. I laughed as humans stumbled over me, tearing their skin and staining me with red as they tried to shelter from the torrential rain. I did not care. They were the ones who carved into my body and murdered others in the woods. But they will see my revenge in the springtime...

Florence Coen (10)

The Wander

It was getting dark. I began to see the dark, mysterious creatures awakening around me. I was lost! It was getting cold and frightening, so I began to run like a panther. Then suddenly, I tripped and fell into a hole. It wasn't any hole, it was the entrance to an evil spirit world. I was worried. I hoped that I wasn't going to be trapped in there like all the other people who had fallen. Then suddenly, something caught my eye. It was a sparkling jewel set in the middle of the Sword of Souls. Finally, my escape.

Kyra Dixon (8)

A Mysterious Hole

Once upon a time, there was a boy named Tom. He was walking through a gloomy and mysterious forest on a murky winter night. Suddenly, he slipped over a puddle and slid down a deadly and gigantic hole. He was so horrified that he couldn't breathe. He was shouting for help but he could only hear spine-chilling silence. All of a sudden, he heard the roar of a lion. The kind lion tried to help him. However, he slipped in the hole as well. Then an angel came and helped them to get out. They became good friends forever.

Shazim Aamir (7)

A Walk In The Woods

When I went to the wood with my mummy, we saw a large clearing and there stood a black animal. Was it a wolf? "No," said Mummy, "it's a black fox."

I said, "It is so lonely and sad." None of the orange foxes were playing with the black fox. "I'm going to give him my cake," I said. I put the cake on a stone. The black fox ate a bit. The other orange foxes wanted some cake too. The black fox nodded. The orange foxes were so happy. From then on, they were friends.

Claudia Castley (8)

Firefly Escape

It was getting dark. The trees shivered, and so did I, as the wind danced its way around the woods. I had been there far too long. Leaves and twigs crunched under my feet as I desperately tried to find my way out with only the moonlight and stars to guide me. Losing what hope and energy I once had, I slumped against the nearest tree, its bark as rough as a crocodile's back. Suddenly, like a million tiny lamps, fireflies lit up the night sky. I gasped in surprise. Maybe I would my find way back home after all!

Javeria Khan (10)

Whispers In The Mist

I'd escaped the horde of Rakulins and saw the lost woods looming over me. As my eyes adjusted, I noticed the outskirts of the woods were engulfed in thick mist. I could hear whispers building up in volume. I froze. Nobody who entered these deadly woods came back alive. I saw a lit torch on a slab of stone. I noticed that the embers were floating down a dark path. It was a sign. I tentatively took my first steps down the path. With my dagger at my side and my wits about me, I ventured deeper into the woods...

Merryn Walker (9)

Lost In The Forest

In a gloomy forest, there lived a small girl named Ashley. Ashley was a very smart girl that thought that she would never get lost, but that thought broke in two. Ashley got lost in the wide, dark forest; she was with her parents at the fair. Ashley asked her mother for an ice cream, so her mother got it for her. When Ashley saw her mum paying, she saw a shining sparkle. She followed it around. It led her into a dark Arctic-like forest. The forest was so cold that Ashley started to sneeze; she was really cold...

Rebecca Ajibade (8)

Scary Adventure In The Woods

It was getting dark and I was in the middle of the woods, drenched in rain.

Then I saw there was an old, creepy castle. I went in without any fear and there were statues, fountains and even old arcade games. I was so pleased to see all of those things. I had an amazing time looking at the scenery inside until the rain stopped.

I would've missed all of that beauty if I was too scared to go inside as the castle looked scary from outside. Never hesitate to go on adventures and discover new things in life.

Sasi Vadan Vemu (7)

Dora And The Lost City Of Gold

Once upon a time, there lived a girl called Dora. One day, Dora went to a forest to hunt for gold, she was really nice and friendly. She found a gold tower which was filled with gold then some guards came and they were very distraught because they thought that Dora was going to destroy the place. Then they trapped Dora. Dora was upset so she called the guards and told them, "I am here for the gold, not to destroy!"

Soon she was let free and they gave her the gold and she lived happily ever after.

Zara Imran (9)

A Wander In The Woods

We are going through the big brass gates, hand in hand. I am Mabel and May is my identical twin. There are people walking their dogs, birds chirping and squirrels running around the place, except for one hidden in a hollow tree. May starts running into the distance. She is sporty, while I normally have my head in a book. The sun is setting and it is getting cold. The fire's starting to be lit. Then we come upon a high tree. May starts to climb, then I hear a scream. May is lying on the ground, not moving...

Megan Ward (10)

Captured

I was lost in a wood when a light flittered towards me and led me to a spaceship. Curiosity got the better of me and I got in.

When it took off, I saw through the window, an emerald green and midnight blue marble with white swirls; I screamed as I realised it was Planet Earth. I was being captured by aliens! Frantically, I ran into the cockpit, fought the aliens and pressed a red button. A thick mist enveloped the cockpit and seconds later, I could see my mum at the exit of the wood. I sighed in relief...

Shiloh Elisabeth Vijayendran

Halloween Night

It was Monday night. It was Halloween. Night was falling. Spirits floated around the dark and empty house. Me and my friends decided to go on a walk in woods as soon as night fell to get into the spooky spirit. The trees were swaying. Darkness was closing in and the path was creeping under our feet. I looked behind me. I was all alone. The sky hurled like it was going to throw up. My mind went into pitch darkness. All was lost. I was stuck in the woods. All alone, nobody with me. Suddenly, it all went black...

Mia Martin (9)

My Dreams

As I opened my eyes, there I was in this magical, enchanted forest. I surely couldn't be dreaming. Lying there in the middle of a big soft, grass field with the sun beaming down at me. As I looked across to my right, I saw elves and fairies jumping and dancing across the rocky pond.

There she stood, her long, silky, blonde hair, a smile like no other, lips as red as roses and teeth as white as snow. Her dress shone as bright as the sun. But little did she know what she was capable of. Is magic real?

Keya Bhundia (9)

The Frightening House

Once upon a time, there was a couple who were tourists. They had arrived in Pennsylvania a day ago. They thought it was beautiful. They went down a road before it got dark and there was a big house, not even a house, a mansion! They were suspicious of houses with locked gates so they ended up leaving as fast as they could.

When they were driving away from the house, they looked at the radio and it was ten o'clock at night. They heard screaming. As they looked back, what they saw was unimaginable...

Michael Barua

Dan's Dreams

Once there was a boy named Dan who went on an adventure in the woods. He saw a bear that chased him out of the forest.

It chased him to his house. He then remembered to play dead so he played dead. The bear turned back to the forest.

Dan woke up to discover it was a dream. He closed his eyes then he fell asleep. The very next morning the events that happened inside his dream, the bear chasing him, him remembering to play dead, all happened. Every day he would wake up to find his dreams came true.

Brooklyn Smith

Lost In The Eerie Woods

The moon was like a silver lamp tossed into the sky as I fought my way through spiky thorns. Time was approaching midnight and I was still not out of the eerie woods. I felt like a new animal in the zoo with all the trees and plants staring at me. The sound of cars and the sight of lights were far away.
Suddenly, I heard a grand squawk up in the sky. I saw the silhouette of a hawk, my favourite animal. It whispered, "Be courageous, you will escape."
It was right. There had to be a way out...

Pin-Chieh Chou (9)

Camping At The Spooky Woods

Once upon a time, there were some campers who went to camp at the spooky woods. Due to lightning, they had to go in a cave and one of the campers got poisoned by their sandwiches! When the lightning was over, a bear charged in the cave. Someone got caught. When they went to camp, a flood appeared. Finally, they made it to safety, then they found a gun and saw a dark figure. They shot it. Then one of the two campers got a knife and killed the other camper, pushing him off the stone into the chaotic water...

Xander Witherow

What A Day In WWI

I heard the shells exploding behind me. I had run into a forest. It was like Heaven compared to what was going on out there. As I ran, I turned around. I saw my best friend, John, behind me, and past him, I could see brave men fighting all those Germans. I knew it was cowardly to run. Suddenly, a blast came from behind me. I threw myself on the ground, so did John. When the dust cleared, I couldn't hear any gunfire or shouting. Just the birds in the trees. The Germans were defeated. Wow. What a day...

Keira Garrs (10)

The Enchanted Forest!

Once upon a time, there was a girl called Zainab. One day, she went on a nature walk. While she was on her nature walk she came across a gate that led into the enchanted forest. First she was asking herself if she should go in or not. She slowly went in and saw big, misty blue fog. As she walked through the fog she shivered. Then she saw so many beautiful animals. These animals had a special power to talk and build amazing cottages. They built a wonderful cottage for Zainab. They lived happily ever after.

Zainab Akter

Hide-And-Seek

One very edgy morning, me and my sister decided to go and play in the abandoned forest. We still went in. It wasn't long before we heard an annoying but mysterious noise. We tried to ignore it. Big mistake. A few seconds later, we chose to play hide-and-seek...

After one round, it was my turn to hide, so I did. I heard the noises from earlier! They were onto my sister. I should have noticed... I immediately went to go and find her... no such luck. I regret that we went there ever since that day.

Eleni Symeonidou (11)

The Dreams Of The Winter Spirit

There was once a boy called John. His family left him to take care of the house. John was resting on his bed when a shiver ran up his spine and he was overwhelmed with fear. Suddenly, a mysterious whisper advised him to go to the forest. His body started to move. His eyelids shut. His heart was beating. After a long period of walking, he had arrived. Then a huge ghostly figure stood in front of him. He cried and whined for help. As he was about to be destroyed, he woke up from his dream. His family came.

Adyan Shahzad

A Wander In The Woods

Something tickled my feet. I opened my eyes to the green canopy above and realised that I was in the mysterious woods. I wandered cluelessly and suddenly stumbled down a deep hole with no way out. It was pitch-black, but I could see a tiny glow. I staggered towards it and I saw a huge triceratops. A shiver ran down my spine. I thought that he was going to attack me, but he pointed towards a narrow path with his sharp horns. Just when I thought I was trapped forever, I saw light at the end of the tunnel!

Nehan Illagolla (7)

Spook Woods

Once upon a time, there were three kids. They were moving to a cottage that was cosy.
One day, they noticed a strange noise. "Come out!" All three kids screamed. "Argh!"
They had a walk. They noticed they were living in the forest. They stepped outside and fell into a lake, drifting far until they saw a magic tree. They called it the Magic Far Away Tree. They were far from home.
They saw a witch and she cast a spell on them and made them rivers all the way home.

Eva Bray (8)

My Nightmare

In the deep, dark woods, a little girl was walking to her grandma's house. When she came out of the woods, she was far away from her house. She was confused and looking to find her way home. All of the people who lived there were turning into animals. One person was gardening and he turned into a horse. The little girl was shivering. She ran as fast as she could. She screamed when she saw a shadow following her in the woods.
She jumped out of the bed when her mum put her hand on her forehead.

Areeba Waqas (9)

The Thing I Shouldn't Have Done

This is the story that changed my life! It was in a deep, dark woods. My friend and I were at camp, we snuck out at 3am. We saw a trail of blood, it pulled us towards it. We heard the trees whispering and screams. We saw bushes moving. A dark figure walked out. He cut my friend's leg. She fell down and grumbled, "Run!"
I ran and looked back, she was pale. I carried on running. She followed. I fell down and the next thing I saw was darkness and that was the last time I saw my friend.

Millie Miller

I Found A Dragon Tree

The stars were out and owls were hooting loudly as I was camping with my parents. Mummy and Daddy were toasting marshmallows.

Suddenly, I heard a roar! A really sad and soft roar. I asked Mummy and Daddy if I could have a little walk in the woods.

After about five or ten minutes, I saw a tree. It was unlike any tree I had ever seen. A twisted tree in the shape of a dragon! Suddenly, the tree breathed gold, blazing fire onto another tree, changing it into a dragon shape! I ran back to my parents!

Walter D'Olier (7)

Experience In The Woods

It was a dark, winter's night. I was alone, walking on the edge of the woods. I decided to go deeper, though it was bound to be the biggest mistake of my life...

While I was going deeper, I heard leaves rustling and sticks cracking, but it wasn't me. At least, it didn't sound like me. Then I heard faint music. Then the fog cleared. The creature twitched... I looked behind me. I thought, *now's my chance to see it!* It was big, dark brown wolf, with the most deadly claws...

Sophie Salmon

Tension In The Fourth Dimension

"Here, boy!" I wandered into the misty woods looking for my puppy, Fetch. It was pitch-black. Twigs crumbled under my feet as I walked further and further into the woods. A speck of light appeared in the darkness of the overlapping trees. I walked towards the light. Suddenly, the ground beneath me crumbled into a pit. An abyss. I knew that it wouldn't be a world of rainbows in there but I closed my eyes and jumped. The trees disappeared and a new world formed around me. A new dimension.

Cressida Bird (9)

The Grey Wolf

I placed my hand on a tree and waited for Lisa to get her breath back. I couldn't believe it. We were in the restricted part of the woods! I couldn't wait to see those bears I saw last week. It was unexpectedly quiet when I heard a noise behind me. With the help of my friend, we parted a few bushes until we came across a grey wolf snarling at us. I knew it was in hunting mode and it seemed famished. Lisa got agitated and began to sprint. Menacingly, the wolf saw its prey and darted at me...

Thanya Uruthrasingam (10)

A Wander In The Woods

I was going for a walk in the woods when I found a trail of pebbles. I decided to follow the trail, so I did. But then, after a few minutes, the trail ended. I was still in the woods. But the thing was, there were ice cream vans, beach balls, sunbeds and the sun was out. I realised that everyone from Spain came into this wood and had a party. They were walking home when I said, "I want to see you again."

They said, "You will see us again." It was really, really mysterious.

Lily Shufflebottom

Nightmare Campsite

I was walking through the woods. It was quiet. I'd lost the rest of the group. They were at the camp. You see, there was a mist and I had been on a walk and got lost. It was getting dark. It must have been midnight. I continued wandering through the dark and gloomy woods when I heard an owl screech. I walked over towards the peculiar noise and saw that I had found my way back to the camp, but it seemed different. It almost seemed empty, but at the same time, it felt like I was being watched...

Mhairi MacDonald (9)

A Wander In The Woods

I stop, I stare. Something's standing right in front of my face. A wood. A massive wood! It looks so eerie but I have to go and explore. As I walk and walk, the golden-orange, rustling leaves fall onto my head. I keep on going, wandering into the woods... I go deeper and deeper into the woods until I find something. No, not something, someone! Then I wait and just look. I look some more but something is running straight at me. "H-ee-ll-p!" But before I can finish my sentence, I am...

Peter Daley (11)

The Midnight Chase

I saw a castle looming over the forest. As soon as I saw the ominous building, every muscle in my body screamed to go back, but I kept moving. Trembling, I knocked on the door. Slowly, it creaked open. I turned, but in a trance, I walked inside. As I walked deeper into the castle, I saw bones scattered. Taking a deep breath, I mustered all the energy I had and dashed away. I ran until I thought I was safe. I sat down behind a tree so it couldn't get me. I felt a sharp pain and then nothing...

Sahasra Veerammagari (10)

The Cottage And The Spirits

Once upon a time, I was in a wood that folks say is an enchanted wood. In front of me was a glowing dot! I followed the path of spirits to a little cottage made from junk food. I looked around for more spirits in case the path led on. There were none. Suddenly, I saw a sign that read: *'Edible'*. I loved candy and all that kind of stuff. I had a sweet tooth, I ate the gingerbread house. Day and night, I ate until I felt like I was about to burst! I went home feeling very jolly.

Alice Peng (7)

The Runaway

As the sun stretched its golden arms one last time, the cruel moon arose. I scrambled through the dense woods and I heard the rats and mice scuttling around me, sending shivers down my spine. The wind howled at me and forced me back. All of a sudden, pain leapt through my body - as I looked down, I saw the iron jaws of a bear trap clenching onto my leg. I thought I had felt pain before but this echoed and ached up to my neck. Suddenly, a man towered over me and offered me his hand. I took it.

Luke Tang

The Forest Nightmare

There once was a girl. She went to bed to go to sleep. Then she woke up to a mysterious, misty forest. Because she was in her sleepwear, she had her teddy which was holding on tight to. Through the gnarled, old roots, she could see eyes staring at her. A shadow slowly but surely began to creep towards her. Then, from the corner of her eye, she saw a sword. She grabbed it and slew the soulless spirit. Then bugs swarmed her. She whacked them out the way and woke up. It was all just a nightmare.

Isabelle Usher (10)

A Wander In The Woods

One day, Charlie was lost in the forest. She was running for her life. Eventually, she found a hat. It looked like a World War 2 army hat. She held it while the trees were rustling. Bushes were shaking because of the loud wind.

Soon, she ran into a man. The man was hunting. He saw her and walked closer and closer. She was scared. He started to shoot. He slipped on mud. At that moment, she remembered the hat. She put it on for protection. Her vision blurred, she felt dizzy and lightheaded...

Liam Kew

A Wander In The Woods

It was a dark and windy night. Jo had decided to go for a walk through the woods. The wind blew against her face. There was the sound of trees whistling in the breeze and a faint call of an owl hooting in the distance. The path got narrower as she went. All of a sudden, she heard a loud, deafening scream coming from behind her. She began to run until she ended up in an eerie graveyard. She tried to find an exit as she wanted to go back home. Suddenly, she felt a cold hand on her shoulder...

Aretha Tsanga (10)

It's Okay To Be Different

It was a cold winter evening. Coming back from football practice, I decided to take a shortcut through a small forest. It started to rain and I had to look for shelter. I found a cave and went inside, but to my great surprise, I found a dragon inside. I was scared but decided to talk to him. I found he was lonely and sad as he breathed ice instead of fire. I assured him that it's okay to be different and decided to make him my friend as he had no one to play with. That made him happy.

Azlan Khalid Noor (9)

A Fairy Door

Once upon a time, I went for a walk in the woods with Dad. I hated walks then. We had reached the middle of the woods when Dad sat down and slept. I crept off when something caught my eye. A door! I touched the wood and suddenly found myself swirling in a whirlwind. I landed unstably and I was surrounded by fairies! I was in a fairy world!
The next few days were bliss until I was whisked back outside the door. Dad was still asleep and I woke him. We walked home and I love walks now!

Amara Mankodi (9)

The Girl And The Turtle

Once upon a time, there was a girl and she lived in a magic forest.

One day, she went to the core of the forest and she found a magic pearl. When she touched it, she could control water. So she turned it into ice that she put in a glass. The girl went to a lake and found a lost turtle. She decided to take it home and give it some medicine. They lived together and helped lost animals. They lived by the sea and had pet fish and went swimming every day. They lived happily ever after.

Rosie Elliott

The Scary Mystery Monster

Me and Charlie, my best friend, were walking in the woods until we got kidnapped by a mystery monster. It was scary, it was midnight. The house was haunted. The mystery monster turned out to be my friend. He betrayed me! Me and Charlie found a way to escape the haunted house, then we had to escape the woods to go back home. Luckily, we did. We thought we were going to be stuck there forever, but no. We made it back home. I was happy, so was Charlie. The whole day was awesome and fun.

Edmund Mwanje (10)

Camp Bear

We went to the forest to find the big, scary bear. One of my friends said the legend wasn't true, but I believed it was. The bear had oak brown fur with yellow teeth, the legend said. So, we were there to find it, take a photo and become famous.

While we were sleeping, we heard a loud roar! We were all shivering. We picked the camera out of the tent and took a photo, but it was on flash. We ran, hid in a tree and sent it to the national bear museum. We were finally famous.

Tony White (9)

The Forest

Once upon a time, I walked into a deep, dark forest and saw a creepy house, a ghost and a campfire. As I walked towards the campfire, I heard a noise behind me. As I turned around, I saw a shadow, so I ran towards the house. I entered the creepy house. There were loads of cobwebs and spiders. I kept hearing noises. I saw a room in the house. I went to look in the room, saw some clown statues and I quickly ran to exit the house. I thought to myself, *There must be a way out.*

Lilly Copley (9)

A Wander In The Woods

One day, I had a wander in the woods. It was almost pitch-black. I walked further still and ahead of me was a dragon! As big as my house! I started running, but nobody can outrun a dragon. Then it put me on its back and flew off! Eventually, we arrived at its cave and I was dropped in a nest. I nearly landed in a baby dragon's mouth! So, I made a run for it and somehow got away! I ran towards the woods, I sprinted through a swamp. I got home and shut my old stained-glass door.

Charlie Turner

The Magical Door

Once upon a time, a girl found a magic door. So she wished that she was in an enchanted forest and then she walked through the door. Then she was there. She went on so many walks.
The next day, she woke up to the magic door so she wished she was in Disney Land and walked through the magic door. Then she was there. She wanted to go on every ride, *but one at a time* she thought. So first, she went on all the spinning cups. Next morning, she woke up in her own bed.

Ella-Dhiya Chauhan

The Woods

I woke up. I caught a quick glimpse of the brunette crows that tweeted a series of loud caws. I heard a plethora of squeaks and rustles, grunts and barks, cries of terror and the wind which whistled around the towering trunks. Tickling my senses were a hint of rotting wood and the taste of the earthy air and damp soil made my mouth water. I experienced a deepening surge of worry and confusion. I began to feel twigs snagging at my hair which blew in the soft breeze not long ago...

Maryam K (10)

Hi Dolly?

Once upon an autumn evening, three girls took a stroll in the woods. A few minutes later one of the girls trod on something bumpy. She picked it up. Creepy, dirty, something that might haunt your soul, like the ones in the movies. They decided to ignore it but weird things started to happen. When they sat down the doll was there. When they climbed a tree the doll was there. Even when they all went home they each saw the same doll in their beds. A day later, the girls were gone...

Sura Lilly (11)

A Wander In The Woods

One day, when I was in the woods with my parents, they allowed me to have a wander around the woods. I set off towards the park to have fun. Suddenly, I felt the ground rumble and shake like an earthquake. Before I knew it, I was falling into a surprisingly deep pit. When I opened my eyes, I thought I was dreaming because I saw the most extraordinary thing I had ever seen: a caveman! I was ever so grateful that he helped me. I was almost in tears! He was so hairy! How wonderful!

Vinudi Gigurawa Gamage (7)

The Hidden World In The Woods

It all started on the evening of the 4th of April when Amy asked her mum if she could take a stroll. After a few minutes of walking, she heard a strange noise. After Amy had passed the entrance of the woods, she was determined to go in. She saw cute, little animals like deer, birds, bear cubs. Amy saw a castle. There were five portals in there. She couldn't believe her eyes! Then when she turned back around, to her surprise, it was gone... Do you think Amy will return home?

Shereen George

A Wander In The Woods

When I arrived at Hatfield Forest, I walked into the woods without hesitating for I was about to embark on an adventure! My lifelong dream of living in the woods was about to come true. I started to make my den in the middle of the forest when I saw a boy. He looked lost and alone, so I welcomed him into my hut for some hot cocoa and gooey cookies that I had warmed on the fire. We became very fond of each other and went on to live a great life together in the woods. Or did we?

Aaron Willis (10)

Bomb

I went on a walk through the woods to get away from the battlefield and the screams and cries. There was a bomb in the town and a tree fell down in the mist, as that happened a person came running past me with a Nazi chasing him. I heard a gunshot so I ran, I looked back and saw crowds of soldiers, some got shot and some ran but then got shot. Then I heard a whistle and recognised the sound of a bomb. I ducked into a ditch, then a German soldier shot me through the heart.

Sammy Norman (11)

No Way Out

She looked back. *Would anyone notice if I didn't go to school today?* She pondered that, having second, even third thoughts! She shook her head violently. "No, Mary!" she cried, reprimanding herself. "If I don't go, they will all think I'm weak." She raced forward, now too far to go back. Taking a deep breath, she edged into the forest and flinched as branches took their turns swiping at her face, missing her face by only inches...

Renah Tamara

A Walk In The Woods

As Jack rustled through the woods at night, he kept going deeper. He couldn't find his way back home. As he walked deeper and deeper, he noticed strange things. Then he noticed a ghost.

They chatted and the ghost told him about the portal in the woods, that he came from. They set off on their journey. They couldn't find it. They saw smoke and a strange glow - it was the portal. He said goodbye and...

"Jack! Wake up! It's time for school!"

Jack Jakaj (9)

A Stroll In The Woods

As I settled down on a comfy looking stump to enjoy my picnic, I was rudely interrupted by the rustle of a bramble bush. I was curious about what it could be. Off I went to have a look.
As I wandered on, I came across a building shaped like a castle. A castle in the woods? I thought that I was losing my mind. However, I was not. So I decided to go on a daring adventure and it seemed to get better by the second! Then I bounded into the castle but could it be a...

Betty Brocklesby Sum (10)

The Mystery Of The Door

Midnight struck. I found myself coming to the end of a mysterious, gloomy forest. I peered down the valley and spotted a door that was surrounded by misty, tall, viny, gross and spine-chilling graves. It was only when I looked next to me, a blood trail appeared. Should I take the blood path? I took the blood path and saw a creepy house. I stopped myself and slid slowly down the side of the valley. I got to the door, opened it and found a world full of dinosaurs.

Oliver Barford (11)

A Wonder In The Woods

One dark night, me and Rosie were asking our mums if we were allowed to go to the woods. My mum and Rosie's mum said yes so we went to the woods. We went to the woods for a while then we went home. Rosie was going to have a sleepover at my house so she got her stuff and came to mine. We got changed and watched a movie. After the movie, we went to bed. When we fell asleep we had a dream we went to the woods for the whole entire night. A creepy dream.

Eshaal Mudassar

The Thing

I heard a noise behind me and was so startled, I ran into the woods. I stopped at an old wicker house and went inside. The door creaked shut and I heard a faint sound as if someone was crying for help, but I thought it was the wind. Being inside an abandoned house was not a pleasant feeling, so I did the most sensible thing, I ran upstairs and into a room. I slammed the door shut. But I was not alone. I was trapped inside the room with the thing...

Harriet Jeffery (8)

A Spooky Camping Site

In the middle of the woods, I woke up because I heard a creepy sound. I grabbed my torch and went to see what it was. I saw a shadow. I didn't know what it was, it was creepy. Then my torch ran out. I was scared. I heard a howl. I went towards it and then heard a noise. I looked back and saw a hurt fox. I gave it food but I was scared it was going to die but I saved it. We became friends but then a pack of wolves came and attacked us.

Ethan Alphonse

The Chase!

Nicolas was on a walk in the woods. Then he found out the forest was enchanted. Nicolas heard a noise and ran towards it. He found a wolf and the wolf started chasing him. He found a cage while running and he trapped the wolf in the cage. After that, he went back to his house and the next day he walked back to the section of the woods and found the cage and threw it off a cliff. He never went there again, he was now scared of the woods!

Sebastian Nodsle (8)

Death Forest

As I walked into the creepy woods, I saw a glimpse of something. Then it charged at me. I ran quickly. It was merely feet away from me. As I looked at it, it had no eyes, only a dark grin. Its body was tall and its nails ended in dark knives.

As I fled to the exit, it slapped my hand with its tentacle. I tried again. I got out. Yes!

After, I got on the bus and went to my house. I got into my bed and fell asleep.

Gurnaman Singh

A Wander In The Woods

I looked at the mysterious woods as I sat and pulled out my goods to enter the woods. I saw a fox wandering across the woods. I gathered my goods and ran into the woods. Now safe from the hound, I explored the woods. Broken branches, dead trees. Someone was watching me. Everywhere. Then I heard the hound. I turned around and heard a growl. Without hesitation, I found a route straight out!

Lucy Rowe (11)

The Enchanted Forest

Once upon a time, above the clouds, hid a forest. Not just any forest, an enchanted, magical, wonderful place. A beautiful forest with fairies, mermaids and magic. Inside, a small village hid where it snowed all the time. It was called Gwyn Eira. The mysterious dreamland was a once-in-a-lifetime gift. If you find it, never leave or you will never find it again.

Elektra Thomas (10)

The Summer Stroll In The Woods

It was a summer's day when I went for a stroll in the woods. I saw birds flying, rabbits hopping and fish jumping in the river. I saw bluebells carpeting the forest floor as sunlight cut through the forest and the world glowed with sunrays. Glancing around at nature's beautiful designs, I felt happiness flood my heart as I knew I was part of nature too.

Enzo Wilson

The Campsite

My name is Aron. It is 1978.

I found an entrance. It was foggy. There was a camp. I ate the plants there. They made me hear noises. Someone was near. I ran and ran but then it stopped.

I saw a cabin and ran into it. I heard a bang on the door and then another bang. The cops came and shot the man. I was okay. The man went to jail. His name was Robert.

Alfie Warriner

A Walk In The Woods

Once upon a time, our family went to the woods. We saw people walking, then a squirrel running up a tree and lastly we saw two horses. We walked a long time in the darkness until we reached the light. At the end of the walk that day my father told me that sometimes in life we need to be brave to walk through darkness in order to reach the light.

Alexia Nyathi (7)

Three Ghosts

Three ghosts were in the woods. Jesus One, Jesus Two, and Jesus Three. Two ghosts were trapped in a cage that takes away their powers. Jesus Three saved them by putting something down which took away the powers.

James Ireland

YOUNG WRITERS INFORMATION

We hope you have enjoyed reading this book – and that you will continue to in the coming years.

If you're a young writer who enjoys reading and creative writing, or the parent of an enthusiastic poet or story writer, visit our website **www.youngwriters.co.uk/subscribe** to join the World of Young Writers and receive news, competitions, writing challenges, tips, articles and giveaways! There is lots to keep budding writers motivated to write!

If you would like to order further copies of this book, or any of our other titles, then please give us a call or order via your online account.

Young Writers
Remus House
Coltsfoot Drive
Peterborough
PE2 9BF
(01733) 890066
info@youngwriters.co.uk

Join in the conversation!
Tips, news, giveaways and much more!

 YoungWritersUK    @YoungWritersCW    @YoungWritersCW